"Unrealized Story in Every Relation between Man & Woman"

"Unrealized Story in Every Relation between Man & Woman"

Indira & Anil

Invincible Publishers

Published by
Invincible Publishers
201A, SAS Tower, Sector 38, Gurugram – 122003
Phone: +91-124-4034247, +91 9355675555
www.i-publish.in

This book is a work of fiction. Names, characters, places and incidents are either the product of the author's imagination or are used fictitiously. Any resemblance to real persons, living or dead, or actual events or locations, is purely coincidental and the publisher does not hold responsibility for the same.

First Published in 2020

ISBN: 978-93-89600-71-1

K. Anil Karthikeya and his wife Dr. Indira are together the co-authors of this book. Karthikeya works with leading steel plants in India. His passion for exploring and conveying concepts which he sees with his vision & hears from his heartfelt thoughts made him walk towards writing "Art of Queen". Dr. Indira is a resident doctor in the Department of Radiation Oncology. They completed this book by sparing around 50 hours in 50 days along with continuation in their respective professions.

Academically, Karthikeya is a graduate in Electrical and Electronics Engineering and has completed postgraduation in Industrial Safety. He is a proud son who thanks his father for every good that happens in his life; thanking him for his practical teachings of life.

The couple spends considerable time with the poorer sections of the society around them to help them enhance their lifestyles.

I humbly express my gratitude and dedication for this narration to

My Father: Late–Shri. **Karri Srinivasa Murthy** Garu

A hero for the world of the past, where future couldn't have created & History can't forget him.

He is a 'synonym for victory, antonym for fear, and an acolyte of Dharma'.

&

Shri. **RATAN TATA** Sir

The Face of Humanity

&

Iconic Director of Indian Cinema
Shri. ***Mani Ratnam*** *Sir*

A classic icon of Indian cinema, an inspiration bridge for two generations of movie makers & creative visualizers.

His vision of creativity & passion for storytelling tells us that age is just a number.

Indira & Anil

Authors Note

"Art of conveying the message in a simpler form is the highest level of intelligence", my father used to say this.

With the same note, we tried to convey this story to you in simple words and framing sentences which can be understood easily.

Narration of this story is simple, honest, classy, raw & emotional. Readers may not get the experience of cosy, sophisticated & dictionary words version.

Men are reliant & Women are creator. Every man reading this is dependent on women in various phases of life with different relations starting from Mother, Sister, Lady Love,

Wife & Daughter. Each of this relation manifests good impact on a Man`s version to this world. You will surely get the essence of the Reliant & Creation chunk after completing this book

To all who agree with us are welcome to explore this book to know how we all are connected.

And to all those who don't agree with us, are most welcome to explore how you can connect to and realize the deeper facets of life and relationships.

Contents

Prologue

"This restaurant is really nice to spend some time," said Mythili to me. I kept quiet and looked into her eyes, her eyes had that charm of achievement. She also started looking into my eyes, her eyes were as if smiling by looking into my eyes, but my eyes were intense somehow. We both kept quiet and continued looking for a few seconds, this was like our souls were kissing with eyes. The charm in her smiling eyes increased, my intense-looking eyes had lost before her smiling eyes, and breaking this kiss, I spoke,

Me: What happened?

She: What happened?

Me: Why are you kissing me with your eyes?

She: I don't know. You started this first and I continued along with the comfort.

Me: No, I was not kissing in the starting, but that charm in your smiling eyes made me lose the intensity in my eyes and I started kissing you.

She: I don't think so. There was no intensity in your eyes, rather I saw some sort of insecurity in your eyes.

Me: (after a pause for few seconds) Yes, you are right.

She: Why Madan, what made you have such insecurities with me?

Me: Maybe, I am wrong Mythili, but,

I am not comfortable with you because mentally, you are much superior to me,

You know every major aspect of my life,

Your concern for me is higher than my concern for you,

Your love for me is like a mountain and my love is like a stone before your mountain-sized love,

You think a lot about my wellbeing,

You are much superior to me in terms of academics & maturity,

You have much better IQ than me,

Your thoughts are much broader than mine,

I am such kind of a guy that I can never let myself down before anyone, I can never approach anyone for any sort of help, but before you, all my skills are not enough to save my skin.

Rather than expecting, I always give the best to everyone, but your normal is even delivering better than my best.

My attitude is like a wall of support to everyone, but your wall of support to me is bigger than mine.

I am superior to the entire world surrounding me, but to me, you are much superior,

I took the concern of many, but never felt the concern for anyone. But now, your love and concern are huger than mine.

I am the best and the greatest in my world, but you are double great than me.

I am saying this to you again, I may be wrong, but I could neither take this nor let you go away from my life. My wanting of you in my life is more than you want me in your life. My intention is not to hurt you, I am trying to get some solution for my insecurities with you because I couldn't get the solution for these. Thus, now I am again dependent on you to bring me out from these insecurities.

She listened to this completely without any word in reply; she took a deep breath and smiled with a light lip movement. The waiter brought the ordered food and kept it on the table. We silently had the food without any discussion. The rocking music and dancing crowd around us were not making any impact on us after my conversation. We just had our dinner while all the people around us were celebrating this moment.

I think I spoiled that evening by opening up myself regarding all this. "Mythili, I am sorry," I conveyed to her while having dinner. She just smiled and replied, "Nothing like that Madan," and continued having her dinner without any word again. I was seeing her eyes now filled with many emotions and slightly watery. I felt bad for opening up on these feelings of mine before her, but at the other corner of my IN ME, it was like, 'Nothing is wrong, you are genuine Madan. You didn't lie to her, nor cheated her, so cheer up and be confident of your honesty in this relation.'

My IN ME started rewinding all those moments and learnings of my life from the school days. I was realizing that most of my learning was with various women with various relations in this life. Starting from my school days, many women teachers taught me the best things apart from education, they taught me well on behaving and communicating. ***Though men are physically strong, women are mentally stronger and clearer than men***, *this may be the reason why most of the schools keep lady teachers than male ones in kindergarten to medium-high school classes*, then came the role of various 'Sirs' who made us disciplined in our lives. Mentally strengthened Women are the base of every initiation and physically strengthened men are protectors of that solid base made by those women in our lives.

Fifteen minutes had elapsed, we were silently having dinner while sitting opposite to each other. The entire confession, I made to her was running in my mind. She was silently having her dinner with emotional drizzled eyes. The music was rocking around us and this celebration mode in the restaurant and those dancing moves to live music was not making any impact on this situation between us. We were just involved in our world of thoughts. I was thinking to have a word with her and start a conversation to divert the intentions and situations that developed in the last thirty minutes.

There was a group of event managers with video recording

cameras and mikes along with an anchor approaching the people in the restaurant randomly and asking kinky random questions related to lifestyle and relationships. This activity made me turn my head towards those questions. After a few minutes, they came to our table and greeted us with a warm smile and kept the mike before me, whereas the cameras focused on me, followed by lighting,

Anchor: What's your name?

Me: Madan.

Anchor: Ok, Mr. Madan. We are conducting promotions of our restaurant on a topic of importance in relationships. Can you and madam take part in this question and answer session with us?

We looked at each other, as we are not talking to each other for a while. Mythili kept quiet and smiled while saying, "Okay."

Anchor: What do you think, in a relationship, who plays the major role?

Me: Both the man and the woman play an equal role.

(The anchor kept the mike in front of Mythili for the same question)

Mythili: As Madan said, both play an equal role.

Anchor: Great. Who actually balances the relation when you have a phase of disturbances or downs?

Me: (This was something near to our situation now) It's a hypothetical question, it depends on the experience. Now the answer varies with case to case, but in most of the relations I have seen, I believe that the Men are Physically stronger and Women are mentally strong. We, men, are like stones in the relationship, whereas women are that sculptors who shape out the stone and work hard to get that beautiful output. We, men, may get frustrated or are fed up after some days in our relationships by losing patience and we feel that all the hardships in the life are because of the woman only. However, we don't realize the woman is that strength and driving force in a relationship which brings out the beautiful output (happy life). Though a woman gives us hardship, a woman gives us the feeling of dominance, a woman may give a sense of superiority over man in a relation, but even she faces the same hardship as us and even takes the same pain as we do. We, men, are mentally weak and expel out easily for some sort of concern from a woman because we feel it as restrictions. Still, a woman is that mentally strong driving force which will hold us, bear with us and take us to the beautiful phase of life.

Anchor: "This is something very great I listened to today," She thanked me for this message and kept the mike towards Mythili and asked, "Mr. Madan had said wonderful lines on balancing a relation and also gave more weightage to women, now please tell us, what according to you brings more respect and charm for you in your relation or for women in any relationship?"

Mythili: In our relation, Madan always gave my space to me and weightage too as you have witnessed in his version, but in any other relation, which I fairly and regularly observe in relations of many of my friends is, "Women must respect each other." Yes, I mean it. In many relations, women are the only enemy of women, men really don't dare to poke or degrade women until and unless other women enter and support the man. That unity among women needs to develop homogeneously and sustain with a respect towards each other, without this we can't expect women will get enough weightage in any relation. Without this respect among each other, we women are always weak and less weighted in any relation.

Anchor: Wow, again that's great listening to you Miss. Mythili. Yes, I totally agree with you. We, Women, need to have respect amongst ourselves, without any scope of getting or giving signs of weakness to men in any relation. She greeted us with the same warm smile and dispersed with the team of camera and lighting.

Now some sort of relaxation was witnessed in Mythili's eyes. She was not so particular about things, but definitely, my version about her dominance caused some discomfort to her. She started looking at me again casually and tried to smile directly by facing me.

Question Bank

Let's have a quick round of few questions, to which you will get answers after completing this narration

Life of a Man starts with a woman giving him birth and it continues to many relations in different phases of his life. **Let's have a quick view of questions you need to get answers to, from this fictional story, for you to contemplate the depth of the narration; in your life and others'.**

In this story, you will witness Madan encountering his Mother; whose love can't be defined with any example, Mrudhula; a junior in college as his ladylove, Mythili; who is the lady of his life, Malini; a prostitute who acted as a torchbearer for Madan and a new born daughter who is significant amongst everyone mentioned above.

How Madan's life got transformed with all these different relations in different phases of his life?

What are those gains Madan got from these women, which couldn't have been gained from the men around him?

What is that important thing a couple must have to live a stable and happy life?

What makes the couple to think out of the box?

What is the better half in a relation of wife & husband?

What are those balancing points in a relationship?

What is that torch-bearing version Madan got from a

prostitute named Malini in Delhi, and how did he get comfort from Malini; how could a prostitute be able to convey that to him and how did he trust her?

What is that Mrudhula had tried to change in Madan during their teen years?

How did his sister transform Madan, and How did Mythili support her sister?

I guess this is a kind of fictional novel where you would find answers simply after not thinking much but experiencing and feeling.

(Around 05:00 a.m. on 02.02.2016)

Women are the creators of this world...Yes, I mean it from now...!

God is supreme having a homogenous power of all the skills & abilities, but the power of Creation chunk in God is solely with the Women.

My **Mother** gave me **Birth,**

My **Sister** brought out **Maturity,**

My **Lady Love** created a **Liberty,**

My **Wife** brought the **Life,**

And, my **Daughter**? I don't know what more she will create in me, but she is one more woman in my life and I surely believe that a creature will come in my life to create what's left in me. This is what is running in my mind with the consequences happened till date in my life. I am Madan, a 29- year-old guy from the shore city & the city of destiny, Vizag, working as a Head in the sales department with a reputed organization in India.

Parallel to my thoughts, I am witnessing a mesh of hurriedness around me which is making my fear reach the next level and is making me panic. I am realizing that this is the weakest moment of my life. There, I see my father, Mr. Murthy in front of me with a warm smile on his face & in a relaxed attire with a calm body language. However, he is witnessing all my panicked senses and is trying to make me comfortable with his attire, by signalling me with half his tongue stuck out, nodding his head slightly and saying that the doctor has discussed about the medical test reports which did not call for anything critical (only parents can make their children feel comfortable in every situation). And, he asks me not to worry and have positive hope.

"Nothing is ridiculous in this world, everything we think & understand matters, my son!" He says. I am listening to every word by standing before him and all the panic mesh is just running in my mind with high doubts, but I am managing to make my appearance as normal as possible.

"Mr. Madan," calls out doctor Ayesha from the Intensive Care Unit (ICU), which is hardly 50 feet distant to me and yes, I am in a hospital. Hospital is a place where the good and bad are equally treated, it is also the only place where the customers never feel comfortable, but never feel troubled too. The strain graph of my brain was increasing with each step while walking towards the doctor. Before I could approach doctor Ayesha, someone calls her and says something which is not audible to me as the distance from where she is called is a bit far to reach the ICU. After listening, the doctor immediately walks out of the room and again, the situation is confined. Two nurses quickly walk into the room, my senses start conveying that the situations are getting worse, which made me worry more and thus panic. My friends and family in the hospital surround me and try to show support with their physical presence outside the ICU room, and at that moment, I look towards my father to feel a self-comfort and see him sitting on a chair in a relaxed attire again, giving out a warm smile. Meanwhile, I am trying to look at the activities happening inside the ICU room through the visible part of a glass door, but nothing is clear to understand, my heart rate is increasing and a feeling of pressure on the heart becomes very heavy after 10 minutes. Doctor Ayesha enters with a smile on her face and wide-opened eyes. Everyone surrounds me, trying to give positive vibes by seeing that smile on the doctor's face, but I am the only one looking at her wide-opened eyes and getting to notice the practical scenario happening inside the ICU. After a while, I understand that the doctor's smile was just to make me relax before revealing something untoward. She keeps a file on my hands and asks to do a signature. I start reading what is in my hands. It is a declaration form for undertaking the sole responsibility in case of any medical failure during the operation. While reading the terms, my eyes shatter with tears not because of the untoward happening but because of the love for my wife.

Yes, I am that husband with my life depended on my wife. I am shivering outside the ICU for my fighting lady inside the ICU. Meanwhile, the doctor completes all the formalities with me, takes my signature and then goes outside the ICU by leaving just a phrase with me "Trust in God". At this moment, I understand how this common phrase, told by the doctors, deals with the hearts of the customers in the hospital.

My ***Heart*** crushed with ***Pressure***

My ***Brain*** loaded with ***Love***

My ***Eyes*** sensed that ***Heat***

My ***Ears*** listened to that ***Heart***

My friends and family are trying to motivate me in all aspects and they are trying to give their support in all the possible ways to make me stronger, but all of a sudden, a voice starts in my heart, saying,

"Hey Idiot, you are a stubborn guy, who had crossed infinite hurdles in life and stood successfully & married your lovely lady,

Yes, she is your wife, she loves you & you love her, You know how strong she is,

Did she ever quit any war?

Whoever be the opponent, Is she an easy lady for the opponent to win?

You are having the world's strongest wife with you,

The higher you get tensed, the more you are degrading your wife, You are the power of the world, but she is the power in

you.

With that conveying of the raised inner voice of my heart, I realize the true power of my lovely partner in my life and now feel myself more practical, more relaxed about the happenings. Then, I slowly walk out of the mesh with which I was surrounded and see my father sitting in a relaxed attire, welcoming me again with a warm smile and he asks, "Is everything okay? You seem to be looking not in a very cool situation, don't worry." I am in a confused state of mind to reply to him with a Yes or No, and start looking at him with a confused expression. He understands my situation and says,

"If yes is the answer, then it's well with the happenings.

And, if no is the answer, then also, it will be very well with the happenings of your life."

After listening to that, now I am again stuck with something more than confusion and staring towards him with a giggling look, I ask him,

"Dear Dad, what do you mean by it? How come it will be very well if the answer is no?" As he is my *baap*, he understands my feelings & sense of confusion, and he replies, "If the situation is not happy, it will be very well, dear son. You will eventually realize why that would be very well."

Again, I start staring at him with more confusion and this time, I open up myself and ask, "How will that be very well? How would I come to realize that in the future? What do you mean by that, Daddy? Do you mean I will be happy without my wife? Do you think that (in a politely raised voice)?" In return, he just smiles, pat on my shoulder and says,

Man is always strong to face anything,

Woman in the life of a man is stronger.

Bonding between both is the strongest ever.

But here,

Your past is the supreme & is as great as ***KARMA.***

He walks away and makes me realize the striking past which

we had together, and which I had in my life till now. This conversation compels me to get into my past & dig into my past with a fresh breeze in my heart, by sitting on a chair at the corner of the floor with sun rays, symbolically welcoming myself in that gorgeous & dangerous past of mine & ours. Yes, the past is not the same for both of us

It was the past for me with the phase when only I was there.

It was the Epic for us in the Phase where we were in it.

Vidyalayam

With a cool breeze in my heart and a relaxed composition of the past in my brain, I am walking steadily towards one corner of the 11th floor in the hospital, where all the corners are surrounded with some good-looking plants, light coloured walls, the pleasant architectural work of interiors and some motivational quotations hanging on the walls. I am busy enjoying all the beautiful stuff surrounding me at this moment, all other people in the hospital on this floor are engaged in their activities and some are tensed for their near & dear ones, but a 6 foot tall man with a super-strong, athletic body is also roaming here, like me, at a distance of 15 meters approximately, and is walking towards me with a smile on his face. I am feeling confused about that man's gesture and I am thinking, "Who is this man coming towards me like a person familiar to me?" Before I complete my thoughts, he comes to me and starts talking to me,

He: Hello sir.

Me: Hello (with a confused look).

He: I have been seeing you from the last 10 minutes, you are so relaxed and pleasant.

Me: Okay, but who are you?

He: Oh sorry...! I am Nishan from Nagpur, working in a video game developing company, here in Vizag.

Me: Nice meeting you, sir (I introduce myself with a casual smile).

Nishan: Great, Mr. Madan, I don't know why but I felt very relaxed after seeing you and your pleasant way of enjoying the atmosphere in the hospital.

Me: That's great of you, Mr. Nishan, by the way, thank you. What are you doing here?

Nishan: My mother is ill and it's a bit complicated with her health. She is under observation in the ICU, after the operation was done in the morning.

Me: Oh sorry, Mister. How is she now? Is everything okay?

Nishan: She is under observation, so I am a bit tensed for the happenings of the next couple of days. By the way, what about you? You are looking so happy, from your face as well as from heart, some good news to share?

Me: No, Mr. Nishan, I was hyper tensed 30 minutes before.

Nishan: Oh, but why?

Me: My wife is admitted here in a medical emergency and is getting treated in the ICU with a high potential of fatal risk.

Nishan: I can't believe this...! Are u serious?

Me: Of course, I was hyper tensed & panicked before 30 minutes, but...

Nishan: But?

Me: I am now relaxed after having a conversation with my father, which made me realize something great & practical stuff of mine related to the past & the present composition of my life. I also felt & realized how great my wife is, and how lucky I am to have her & how heroic she is.

Nishan: Great listening done, Mr. Madan. Now I can see your pleasant pleasure, even from your eyes too.

Me: Thank you, Mr. Nishan, it was nice meeting you.

Our conversation ended with one more impact on me by feeling the difference between the most panicked moment of my life before 30 minutes and this pleasant moment now, where a stranger felt and explained it with a glad gesture.

Now, I stop enjoying the mesh around me, start walking towards a corner where the rays of the sun were passing through a window and hitting my heart resembling how my eyesight used to do so on that lovely lady from my past college days, which took me to the decade before.

(July 2005)

Visakhapatnam, this shore city is traditionally known as the Jewel of the east coast with an urban population of 2.5 million and with signs of peace among the top 10 GDP cities in India. Also, it is the only city in India with two major ports, a primary Integrated steel plant, an oil refinery, power generation units, armed manufacturing unit, and scenic beaches.

There are 16 beaches in this place which is the highest number of beaches after that of Goa in India. One amongst the sixteen beaches is the Yarada beach; the beautiful scenic beach, with the track record of being the safest.

V. Vidyalayam is a residential college located approximately 500 meters away from the beach, in an area of 22 acres, rich in horticulture, high in culture and is well known as the temple of education. It is a home of discipline & ethics *(students over here are appraised for their ethics and discipline than their academic excellence).*

It is an ethical campus in a peace-minded environment in the most peaceful city. Yes, we can assume the philosophy of the campus is purely adopted from the core style of the city; in a simple way to elaborate, the campus is the manifestation of the city culture.

Back in July 2005, I was a student at V. Vidyalayam, in the Final year of *Mechanical Engineering department.*

The location of the college canteen was in a big room of 60 x 90 square feet. It was a big, centralized air-conditioned hall with pleasant instrumental music tweaking all the time, and it was located at hardly 300 meters away from the seashore. Just imagine the visuals from our first home in the college only 300 meters from the seashore, which obviously makes a student turn into a thoughtful leader involving certain activities of both, the good & the bad *(good & bad alters from person to person and it is the same which I sense every time in every activity I do & I go with).*

Inside the canteen, there were arranged, with the professional architecture of blue and white coloured walls, some legendary personalities' photographs with quotations and the rare achievements of our college. The set of tables and chairs in the canteen were arranged in 7 rows and 15 sets in each row, in total consisting of 105 sets, where rows were consequently marked; starting from to V1 to V7, where our rebel group got a constant place in the canteen, which was exclusively settled in the east-facing beachside where sun rays directly struck on us.

We were a group of 22 rebels in the college campus, setting everything on track when things were off track at the college, and the canteen was where the issues which couldn't be raised open to air came to us, the rebels. Ethical judgment would be given by an unethical process *(yes, you are assuming correct, it's something like the idea of goons in the society and crazy rebel guys in college, but the difference is* ***we were notorious as per our college ethical principles, but were practically acceptable from the hearts in the campus****)*. It was not something like a passion for us to make groups and do time pass and whatever we like, and it was not at all an unethical business by our team; it was purely a rebel group united on the ground of the sensitive issues getting raised to the core and heat inside the hearts ignited from the majority of the hearts; resulting in huge support for our rebels. Yes, you are getting it right, in the history of this 31-year-old ethical based college, one had never come across such a notorious group.

(Robin Hood had alone created a remarkable impact in service for the needy in the past. Here, our rebels was established from

the ethical issues prevailing due to unethical people.)

None of our senior batches or college staff had thought of this till now, because of the ethics and discipline in the college. If they did so, they would be terminated from the campus as per the disciplinary policy of our college, but still, we were managed, kept, supported, and raised by all, including our principal also, because of the sole reason that we were always bounded within the policies of our college. The issues related to our college & surrounding village issues connected to the campus, which could not come out to the light and get settled, would be moved on to our desk.

We, 22 rebels, didn't know whether we were right or wrong, but we were fairly going onward with uprightness as our parents taught/ made us live since childhood. No one amongst us was handy with each other before bonding for these sensitive issues. The positive aspect of us Rebels was the UNITY. Although many big seeds tried to divide and separate us by creating rifts but the Unity among us made our Rebels stand strong. All the big seeds tried their level best with all the silly and false allegations on us, to bring us out as negative among the public in college, but only the unity in us, the Rebels, made every allegation proved wrong. We gained more trust in the campus which made us more answerable.

Slowly days were passing with these mesh & rush activities. One day, a circular was released in the college for a drive on social cause for which the entire campus needed to come forward for a campaign on saving the girl child at Athreya foundations at Vizag on 23rd July 2005. It was scheduled at 8:30 am with all the associated volunteers and our campus students.

That was the day, 23rd July 2005. My day usually started with a song from one of the music systems in my surroundings. It shattered my dreams in sleep, exhausted that feeling & manifested the life again with one more day; with an incessant unpleasant mood. But, that day, I pleasantly opened my eyes and found myself below a mango tree. I felt very much surprised by how I was there, when did I go there without my knowledge? I was just trying to recollect all the happenings that happened in the just past, but nowhere, I was getting any idea of how I got there. I heard the voice of my father saying, "in the midnight, there was a power cut from 2 am to 4 am and in the meantime, you shifted here for better sleep." Again, I realized the magic of my dreams in the past night and started feeling the Giga of the pleasantness of the girl in my dreams, which made me rethink the dream, by seeing that beautifully placed couple of mangoes hanging from a tree, which were diagonally settled, also parallel to this recollection from my fantasy of dreams.

I heard the music of an 8 am-news program from our TV inside the house which made me understand the time being 8 am and I remembered the program at Athreya foundation scheduled for 8:30 am, and in rush with a thought of attending the program, I jumped out from the cot.

By 8:05 am, I was done with trimming my beard & levelling moustache (Symbol of Royalty for men).

By 8:10 am, I was out of the bathroom after all refreshing activities (Just one newly released Telugu song playing on my Bluetooth speaker is enough).

By 8:12 am, I was ready with attire (imagining the other part of the day with my heart).

By 8:15 am, I finished my breakfast (by communicating to the REBELS group about the spot of the meeting).

By 8:17 am, I started my Royal Enfield (Like a LION riding on a Black Indian Horse).

At 8:25 am, all REBELS met at the place & were ready for a drive to the campaign at Athreya Foundation. At 8:31 am, we were in the office of Athreya Foundation which is a hilltop beachside campus.

The astonishing campus was covered in dense greenery which always imparted a sense of cosiness to my eyes. Blossoming flowers were spreading fragrance and dancing with the wind as if emulating a wave on the seashore. The walkways were marked in a nostalgic disciplined manner, reminiscent of my formative years, sending my conscience back to the younger me holding a heavy school bag with a water bottle. The sea breeze shook hands with the warmth of the sun, making the trees wave at me with frantic emotions as if asking me to hug them. My mind instantly visualized a rainbow in the same clichéd manner that we used to draw in the 'the scenery' in our childhood days.

I opened my hands widely, facing towards the sky with my eyes closed & sense of joy flowing from my heart, enjoying the beautiful ambience of the campus with a feeling of comfort and joy. I had exactly engaged myself in the joy of my giggling heart with core satisfaction after a long- long period in my life *(I don't know why God gives a joyous moment before an awesome phase of our life & sad news before starting a tragic phase in life).* But this time, I felt it truly by listening to "*Heyyy Mrudhula*, here we are," from some corner of the campus I was in. I didn't know that a voice from some corner of the campus would soon turn into an echo in my heart. Coming out of my fantasy world to this materialistic jungle, I tried to turn my head to that corner where the imminent echo was coming from & witnessed a Masakali (Pigeon). It was flying in front of my eyes, and I wanted to find out what magic was happening around me; it was a feeling, such sweet & cool.

There, I saw a beautiful lady, following that lovely Masakali, running on her gentle toes, chasing eyes & flying heart. Watching her run was like a rainbow running before me (all the pleasant environment around me shifted to her twinkling beauty & pigeon in the scenario, with that running rainbow completing my soul).

Dancing in the rain of happiness

Stood like a dream before my eyes

Surprised with the beauty I witnessed

An affectionate lust started in my Heart

Heartbeat started jumping like waves in the sea

Signs of sleepless nights hitting my thoughts

Big magic waves hitting my aura from her smile

Realizing the surprise of seeing a thunder flash of beauty before me

Core Soul signalling my brain on leaving my body for a while to fly around her fragrance

That was the first frame of her in my life which made an impression for the rest of my future (how silly I was, but I loved to be silly for her), which was reflected in my actions:

Her ***running toes*** *with my* ***unbalanced feet***
Her ***chasing eyes*** *with my* ***exhausted eyes***
Her ***flying heart*** *with my* ***freezing heart***

After a minute of my first mesmerized journey; there came a gang of ladies surrounding her with smiles, praising her for catching the flying Masakali. Then started a gala conversation which seemed like resuming a paused discussion between them, making it tougher to crack on what discussion was going on between them,

Friend 1: Masakali is with her Masakali.

Friend 2: No, it's a junior with its senior.

She: *No. It's My Soul with My heart.*

That made the second echo cracking in the core of my heart, first realized with the first echo "Hey Mrudhula" (about a moment ago). Was she the one who raised a quake inside my heart& started residing in my heart? That's me, again going crazy with her voice; it was like doing a bungee jump from a top cliff for the first time, after a while of which, I tried to figure out the sense of stating,

"It's My Soul with My Heart." I found a sillier, interesting & a person crazier than me. At that moment, I found that the names of both My Lady Love & Masakali were the same. Yes, she was Mrudhula.

'Ms. Mrudhula Krishna' kept her name to her Masakali, with the love for birds she had. After the rest of the conversation, I came to know Masakali was left free without any imprisonment & restrictions. I was also surprised to heart that she was maintaining a home for Masakali in her home & let it rest daily. I could listen to all this clearly because it was a group of girls discussing over; of course, you may know the noisy impact & innocence in the gala of gang of ladies but their excitement added the impact to make it doubly audible which converted the entire story into an arrow injecting into my heart. Meanwhile, pleasant music was hitting my ears like a background score for the happening scenario, but after enjoying it for a bit, I realized it was my ringtone and I was getting a call from an unknown number. I picked up the call, "it's Rihan" in a vexed, hurried tone. I sensed some bad indications which struck the tensing chord of my brain. I responded with a *'hello'* & *'yes'*. Rihan told me to run to a hospital & before that reach to the blood banks nearby me because Vijay, the stout looking mate in our group was injured badly by someone. As a result, O negative blood was an immediate requirement. This shocked my senses with a wave of high anger & pain, after hearing that Vijay was injured by someone. I was at a stage of being unable to recognize the transformation from love to anger in just half a minute, feeling like I have lost all the senses & I was running with a destructive vision to see the end rather than saving the situation and without my notice, I hit the table beside me which hit some stranger badly. I couldn't even recognize that but framed it partially in my mind. I was running like a football player to hit the goal for satisfying the ego in me. When I reach the Indian hospital at clock town junction, my common sense reached to such a level that I couldn't spare a second for myself to think & act to ask the details at the reception counter; rather I just followed the heat in the core of my heart & the glare of my eyes. I just followed all the known factors to reach the destination; the system running inside me at that moment was awe-stuck to heat in the heart & findings of my eyes. I was just witnessing all the surroundings known to me one after another & I was walking on that path. I didn't know where it was leading, but my senses were running & my legs were walking unsteadily. At last, somehow, I reached the room and saw Rihan beside a door and the parents of Vijay beside Rihan. His mother was so tormented that she wasn't able to even raise her eyes, and his father was a bit angry with me which was clear from his eyes & facial expressions. It brought me a feeling of guilt, making my anger to rise high and my hands were dirty with grease. I completely had no idea how it happened. Meanwhile, I was trying to figure out how the grease came to my hands, in parallel, searching for some water tap. I found a washbasin with a tap. I pressed each tap for flow of water, which was for a few seconds, but couldn't manage to clean the grease after 3 pressings too. I understood it couldn't be cleaned with these breakages in flow, but as I did not have other options to clean the grease, I started to think of other alternative ways to clean, while seeing my face in the mirror & hands under the tap with flowing water.

Sensing someone standing aside me, (it was like my aura was feeling very uncomfortable and it was as if some other aura was entering into my comfort zone,) I turned the head to my right side. To my surprise, it was Mrudhula standing beside me to hold the tap continuously to get enough water flow.

I didn't know if it was strange or a routine. I was feeling like a heavy-hearted guy with the pleasure of a fragrance coming from the presence of Mrudhula. She, being very close to me, made me feel uncomfortable in my own aura; all these thoughts splashed like a spark in seconds. I tried to connect with her eyes by conveying the level of innocence through my eyes. As a result, to my surprise, I got a gesture from her eyes, by her, closing them for a second & nodding her head down with a beautiful smile on her lips. I started recollecting the change in phases of my mind in the last 10 minutes; how the red-hot smoke occupied my aura, how bad and evil captured my heart, and how uncomfortable & imbalanced I was, when Mrudhula entered in my aura. In parallel to these thoughts, the eyes of my senses started opening and kept a question before me; "She is the lady of your heart, your heart had drowned below her feet an hour ago, she is here without your knowledge; what fantasy is acting with the life; how all these laws of life are acting on you within a short span?"

I was completely clueless in my thoughts but there resulted a conversation between us,

She: *"Clean yourself first"*

Me: An unanswered, confusing question was solved as she triggered the best moment in my heart. Keeping myself quiet, I unknowingly obeyed her; completed cleaning my hands & then started staring at her without any reply.

She: You have cleaned yourself on the OUTSIDE, not on the INSIDE.

I started staring at her again with an unanswered expression and a confused look.

She: The grease on your hand is cleared, but not the anger & agony in your heart.

I started smiling by maintaining eye contact with her.

She stared with an innocent and confused look & couldn't trigger the reason behind my intention to smile as the intensity in my smile was rising with the pitch & it was leading to a sarcastic sort of scenario.

In an instant, we noticed the medical staff moving around hurriedly by leaving hints for an abnormal condition. Mrudhula gets a bit confused by seeing the situation; what I could sense from her facial expressions was the manifestation of a full moon glow in panic. Witnessing police behind me, she asked me to turn. Mr. Ranjan, the regional inspector of Visakhapatnam, stood with his back towards me with a document in his hand. I formally greeted him with a smile, he revealed the scenario of our college and how he collected evidence of the attack by bad seeds who tried to attack us. With a gesture, he thanked me for a timely response and making arrangements after getting complaints from the local people and by how presenting eyewitnesses made the problem solved in quick time & punished bad seeds behind this which manifested justice. Mrudhula, after witnessing this conversation, felt surprised of the happenings before her,

She: I am sorry for my views.

Me: What happened?

She: Let me get an excuse from you first.

This time, I understood her intentions, which made me stop feeling unanswered.

With a surprise & an answering appearance, she clasped my intention of kindness.

I started looking at my other side.

She: How can Mr. Ranjan thank you when you created the violence & took law & order in your hands?

Me: In the same way you asked to get an excuse from me after getting my intention. Similarly, he had responded by coming here, the only entity here is the belief on the rebels & unity of the rebels, and if we don't do the needful on time, this could create pain for one more family in a nearby village.

She: How can you justify this in your perception?

I started explaining her the roots of our rebels, how our rebels were accepted in the hearts of masters in the campus by balancing the ethical code of this historic college; 5 years ago, the local politicians of the city had a lack of students' support, who are utmost useful for their political growth. Thus, subsequently, they planned to have this support from one of the most respectful colleges like V Vidyalayam, which could add some neutral voters' positive impressions for them. Our college fame got stuck in such a trap where our management couldn't go ahead with such selfish people anymore, hence, we stayed calm. But this softness gave them a cushion of acceptance and they started their notorious activities in nearby villages, which started to affect the reputation of our college and security in the nearby villages, these instincts had resulted in the roots of rebels in college.

She: You can call me Mrudhula.

Me: Okay.

She: How did the management leave you guys, without handing you to the police?

Me: There are double-digits of incidents which had occurred in the last couple of years, where the police & local villagers were affected personally and today, 16 of us were raised from the instincts which surfaced.

She: What are those instincts? I never have heard any of them.

Me: You may have heard of those, but you may not be aware of the if's & but's of those. The problem is not with you, the problem is with the perceptions which we make so early, even before releasing carbon dioxide from us. We don't show much interest in reading the news but the headlines, the same is the cause of creating the roots of these bad seeds in our city from our college.

She: Hold down, start calling me Mrudhula.

Me: Okay, but it takes time to do so.

She: Is it so? Why would this take time for the rebels like

you who can acceptably tackle those goons in an acceptable manner by college ethics code?

Me: Stop calling them goons, they are not goons. They are just used by politicians for their benefits & the bad part is they do not realize this and have just surrendered themselves to have some money for their fantasies and luxuries. We intend to make this realization with little violence (if required) and get them out from the clutches of those selfish leaders. And make note of one thing. I am not handling them. We Rebels are handling them.

Divya, who was listening to all this by standing at the side of Mrudhula, interrupted this conversation and stated,

"We always witnessed, heard much about your violence than making a change. In fact, we never dare to see you guys directly on this campus, and having a word with you to share some problems is the far distant thing to happen. We girls have a fear to face your team of rebels."

"So, you know about those bad seeds?"

"Yes," was the answer by Divya.

"Do you know the incidents which have happened in the village?"

"Yes," was the answer by Divya.

"Do you know what justice had been done to those victims?"
"Yes," was the answer by Divya.

"Then, what best can we do other than this? We are not here to impress someone; we must shape our future with the knowledge from our college and score good grades. The things which you know/ heard about us are just our passions to return something to our society, we feel and believe in returning the good to the society rather than expecting the good to happen."

Mrudhula: It was like a 'wow' to listen to these intentions from people in this society. I would love to explore more about you.

I was shocked to hear this from her. An hour back, I was dreaming to listen to her voice, watch her smiling for some more seconds and now that lady had herself expressed to know more about me and would love to talk to me. This was like a dream come true, the feeling was like I am the captain of the ship standing on the top deck with her and watching the super moon on one cool breezy night in the middle of the ocean. Coming out from the fantasy of happiness and thankfulness for my father for giving this best character which I feel proud of, I gently left a smile from my eyes and tried to stare at her politely, and asked her to pinch on my hands,

"Mrudhula Krishna..." I called her.

"Wow, at last, you called my name," She said.

"Can you change it to Mrudhula Madan?"

(Silence across the globe started surrounding me)

Divya was trying to interrupt the silence by saying something. But in parallel, my brain & heart started shivering with fear of enthusiasm with thoughts between yes or no, and breaking all these, Mrudhula reacted on her name, saying, "It's Mrudhula Krishna" & she walked away, followed by Divya.

With no clue other than this, I stood for some minutes and thought to come out of the disaster which had just happened. No signs of damage preventions were striking my mind.

I started cursing myself for how daring I am, from where this daringness jumped in me; from looking at the lady with fear to proposing the lady to come into my life, from thanking my father for giving me the best character to cursing myself for daring in front of her, without a second thought.

Still, my mind & heart maintained steady rates of strain graph and they started convincing each other that no mistake had occurred in this scenario, my heart started appreciating my brain on conveying the honest feeling of what it has and the brain started defending by backing my character for what I feel proud of; that I never cheated any other heart even in my thoughts and I never dared to think of sharing my life with another heart. So, what is the big deal here in proposing my genuine intention towards her, in fact, my mouth did the right thing by conveying what the heart felt, in the right time rather than keeping it till the moment where the heart starts bleeding.

Hold on, please, I stopped all this conversation in me and started kicking my heart with a closed wrist and started questioning, was this the right moment to share the feelings? Genuinely, I felt we may conclude things by ourselves, but 'what she might think', was the question running in my head.

What her IN family would like in me, what suggestions her IN family will give, my heart was in a little dilemma after thinking about all these questions and now my mind started dominating by saying, 'don't worry, with honesty in our family we unitedly are capable enough to dominate any other IN family.'

Still, I was not convinced, I started thinking of her IN family situation then. What may the conclusions & questions be, in her IN family right now? Will her IN family at least consider my proposal? Or will it take my proposal very casually? Or is there any tie-up existing with any other IN family? These questions were all that I could think at the moment.

My IN Family started raising voice by keeping base on my heart's honesty and mind's self-supremacy.

The IN Family... (IN ME)

IN FAMILY includes the self's brain and heart and the inner instinct expressed through eyes. These play a vital role in my day to day presentation/ communication; I diplomatically balance my IN family & try to read the others' IN family.

The clock ticked to 9 pm and like every day, I was listening to music on the television in my home. The 9 pm news bulletin was about to start, but that day, I was not interested to know what is the news or what is going on in the globe surrounding me. I was dipped in the thoughts of the morning magic which happened & the quake created by my IN family.

A new message was getting displayed on the lock screen of my Nokia 3110. I opened the message, with no interest; it was about the date & schedule of the upcoming annual fest of the college. My IN family jumped into the scene again and began making some plans to interact with her. If interaction or conversation would not be possible, then at least, I wanted to read her IN family by secretly looking at her from some corner. Based on her body language, we can have a conclusion about the impact of the proposal, keeping all these thoughts in my mind I fell asleep. The next morning, I checked my mobile to see if there was any update about yesterday's happenings, but nothing was triggered anew. I started my day travel, ahead to the hospital to have a casual visit to check Vijay and planned to check in the college with some dilemma about her IN Family.

Divya: Do you know, Madan was attacked thrice by the local politicians last year?

Mrudhula: Who is Madan, why was he attacked?

Divya: Hey Ram, you are asking who is Madan; he is your Krishna.

Mrudhula: Mrudhula is for Krishna, not for Madan.

Divya: So, are you responding to yesterday's proposal of *Mrudhula Krishna to Mrudhula Madan?*

Mrudhula: I don't know how you took the condition, but my intentions are clear, I am the dearest daughter of a highly respected gentleman, Mr. Krishna, so I can't think to risk his hard-earned esteemed fame. In my life, I am still not done with my studies, I seriously believe that *I can discuss these things, but cannot decide.*

Divya interrupted her & started resisting by conveying some practical, mature advice of the age. "Why are you restricting yourself by drawing circles around you?"

With a bit bold voice, Mrudhula rose on Divya, "Even I know, at this point of age, all these things may not be the need of the hour, but this is the major aspect for every woman to select the best man for the rest of her life, there is nothing called love, marriage, blah blah. With my practical senses, I believe every relation, excluding blood relations, is just a sort of business deal only, every creature starts the relation with some gains or trades in any matter & just to balance them accordingly is the basic step of longevity in the relation. Even I know this well, but in my view, I am not ready," Saying this, Mrudhula started walking towards the road with a pitch of anger. Divya followed Mrudhula.

Mrudhula saw a few children on MG Road, engaged with some others in a group of labour activities which diverted the anger & discussion towards the tone of mercy and sympathy towards children.

Mrudhula felt much disturbed from the discussion that happened a while before, and now with the new visual scenario before her, she started to think of the causes of deploying children in work & background of their family conditions which lead to these. Mental sickness acquired her heart & mind. Divya interrupted her thoughts by stating that the attacks happened on Madan thrice last year, because of this Child labour only.

Divya: Local politicians started this sort of business by engaging children in labour works and not letting them go to school; keeping their futures hanging in the air.

Mrudhula: How is Madan involved in this?

Divya: Hey Ram... You just started hating him without a reason. You, yourself, started loving his ideology and concerns towards social issues yesterday, while he was conveying the passion of Rebels in our college. And now, you are in a thought to ignore him.

Mrudhula: Does this make any sense?

Divya: It does, we know rebels' batch in our college rescued 79 children from this child labour mafia from the local politicians. Also, once we witnessed a big fight in our college between rebels and the bad seeds, who were supported by the local politicians; because the Rebels cracked the child labour deployed illegally. One night, Madan was driving alone on this MG Road and got attacked by more than 30 goons, resulting in critical injuries.

Mrudhula: I had heard this, but I was not aware of who got attacked. "We come to conclusions so early" is what Madan said yesterday; "we decide before we even release carbon dioxide from us."

(In the Indian Hospital)

I took the discharge certificate of Vijay from the doctor's hand. Vijay's father walked towards me and thus made my stress graph bit high because he was a fighter for social & anti-national issues in his student days of life. Of course, *we were his past versions & he is our next version,* he could witness what we were not able to witness in us, we valued his words of experience, but I never understood why he didn't accept our passion of fighting against the bad seeds around us.

(Fest day in College, August 5th, 2005)

Fest mode was manifested from the entrance gate of the college. Many colourful clothes, banners, and papers were kept in different places of walls & pillars in the college. There was no uniform that day, most of the students were in civil dresses and maximum unofficial couples in college were trying to bring out their fashion sense to impress their dearly loved ones.

My eyes which had lost the vision of dreams from last night started searching her.

I slowly proceeded towards the stalls section where mini entrepreneurs of India were witnessed. We, the rebels, were very much interested to explore the stalls arranged, but I was least interested to explore the stalls because the fellow students always showed some bloody fear of respect for the rebels, due to which I felt much uncomfortable. The destination in my thoughts was nowhere near to my vision, my aura started feeling scratchy due to the fear of respect we were receiving, and I decided to move away from these stalls to search my destination in thoughts.

My eyes sparkled with her face as I turned to 2'o clock position, immediately, I turned to my 8'o clock position where I got the destination of my thoughts. Mrudhula was the vocal message sent to my mind from my heart, bypassing my mouth. My heart started dancing with soft Goosebumps in eyes & the impact of stress in my legs made my feet to walk towards her.

"What are you doing here amidst stalls?" I asked her. She kept silent without a reply with her head down towards a table in the stall. "We have put up a food stall in this fest," answered

Divya from behind, and Mrudhula raised her looks from the table towards Divya.

I was thrilled to get my voice raised before her & my 'In Me' started to conquer. Generally, I have a bold version with a rough voice every time with everyone, but I used a soft speaking version towards Mrudhula.

But now, my voice was getting raised in front of her, this made me thrilled. I continued raising my voice.

"What would you get from this stall in the fest, why to stand here for a long time to provide some food service to someone, why are you damaging your reputation? You are very precious in my world & my world is very precious to me & my thoughts are better superior to the thoughts of others around me. Please, just come out of all this stuff to make yourself high before me in my world."

"How can we cancel this after investing good time and amount?" said Divya again from behind.

"We can't compensate for your invested time; can you please give me 100 food tokens of your stall? We need the food from your stall," said Rihan by cutting Divya's words in the middle. Divya got surprised after listening to the 100 food coupons' order from Rihan. I was playing the lead from the crowd, staring at Mrudhula & witnessing the conversation happening between Divya & Rihan.

Divya: Our stall hardly has 120 food coupons; how can we give 100 coupons to you?

Rihan: It doesn't matter. We need all 120 food coupons; we will have some purposeful work with those 120 food coupons than what you are doing here.

Divya: There are other food stalls also here, right? Why can't you take from there too?

Rihan: Excuse me, Miss Future Entrepreneur of India, we are concerned about the food you sell here & much more concerned about Mrudhula standing here in this crowded fest.

Divya: Fest is in the college, right? She belongs to this college only, right? She stays here and she roams here daily, in this crowd only, right?

Rihan: Those were the days when Madan didn't reach his destiny. Now, the gears are different. We, the Rebels, are on the pitch of our college & at attention to the locals & precious for our supporters. For us, Madan is the Chief and Mrudhula is a possession of Madan now.

Divya: Excuse me.

Rihan: Don't worry, we respect your views & thoughts, Divya. We need all those 120 food coupons you have.

Divya: What will you do with those, what is that noble work you are going to do?

Rihan took the coupons from Divya & handed them to me with a smile, I handed those coupons to Mrudhula, kept my hands on her shoulders with a feeling as if I had got my destiny & my destiny was in my hands. Parallel to this, Rihan gathered all the 22 rebels in the fest to collect those coupons from Mrudhula. She was confusedly comfortable with the previous conversation & the present happenings before her. All the rebels collected those 120 coupons & Rihan handed the money of those 120 coupons to Divya and asked her to shut the stall without any cross-questioning. Divya shut the stall, some enthusiasm jumped in her IN ME to explore the utilization of the collected food, and without asking about the utilization of the food, Divya quietly went behind the rebels. The rebels were on their way to take the food & Divya followed them quietly with a question bank in her mind. The crowd related to my world soon dispersed from the stall, as I comfortably proceeded with Mrudhula.

"What do you think of yourself? What was that conversation of Rihan with my friend? Don't you think that thoughts and intentions can miscommunicate the senses? In addition to this, you were trying to place your hands on my shoulders comfortably when I was in a state of confusion, don't you have a minimum thought of my comfort?"

I tried to keep my hands back on her shoulders again, and her continuous murmuring picked a high intensity. Her words got harder and cheeks turned like the red moon. By tossing away my wrist, she got rid of my hands from her shoulders. My 'IN ME' started celebrating the sense of victory in conquering her 'IN ME'.

Bad Seeds

As the local body elections were approaching, the bad seeds in the fest were trying to get the mileage by starting their malice & malevolent doings with other students on the campus. From the corner of my eyes, I observed that 3 girls from the chemical engineering department, with one faculty member, were standing on the side of a pillar, worried and with a tensed expression on their faces. I came out from the thoughts of mischievous discussion with Mrudhula and the happy state of 'walking on a rainbow' & turned towards the chemical engineering department, towards them. There were 3 bad seeds teasing them by provoking and extorting them with some words which were not audible to me as I was a little away. I went behind them, greeted that faculty who was trapped up along with 3 girls among the Bad seeds. I kept my hands on their shoulders, made them stand at the corner pillar which was approximately 5 meters away from Vicky (pro in the bad seeds batch & nephew of the state minister). He was the link between the bad seeds in college & the local politicians. Vicky was the core origin of ruckus created on the campus. The founder of this ethical temple, V. Vidyalayam was Mr. Nayak, he also didn't have the guts in his spine to stop these ruckus activities because of his clean image; he was the most respected & soft-hearted person with a bright image in the society, but his image was one of the root causes for the origin & rise of the bad seeds in the campus. There is a quotation which strikes me commonly when I remember him, ***"You can't raise your voice when you are in a Glass-House."***

That is, when we build & maintain a glasshouse, we are unfit to raise the voice. This turned out to be oxygen for the bad seeds & intentions of those behind them.

The rise of rebels in the campus was parallel to rise of people with bad intentions behind the bad seeds. Excluding Vicky, everyone from their team was innocently trapped with luxury, false fame & alcohol. False fame was the key factor for guys at that age to get attracted without realizing that they were involved with people having bad intentions. So, we never tried to target them or blame them. After hearing of any issue in the campus, we tried to think maturely by not involving all the bad seeds into the picture, we tried to figure out the loop because of whom the actual deviation occurred and then Vicky & the politicians behind them were found guilty in most cases.

Meanwhile, one girl among those 3 girls started crying out with vexation to vent out her pain. By seeing this, Vicky got alerted to avoid highlighting the issue and tried to control the situation by pushing me aside. Vicky started shouting loudly on the girl, trying to create a panic situation in the nearby surroundings in the campus, and he tried to call the bad seeds who were visible in his vision nearby, to stand by his side. Vicky's panic started increasing after seeing me smiling confidently with a lot of sarcasm. In a hurry to save himself & controlling the situation around us, he held my shirt's collar and tried to look angry. But, an expression of fear was visible rather than anger in his eyes. I started smiling more broadly with more confidence than before.

He started shouting after seeing my confident smile which got broader now. I guess that intense confidence of mine hit him badly because I was sure he knew me well in the way of these fistfights and chain fights in the campus. I was alone, very well capable of handling the anger of horses in the college, but no horse could cross before me when my anger touched the saturation point.

The God & Man spirits inside me met rarely to avoid that destruction when some injustice or unavoidable situations arose. This time, Vicky slapped that girl to make her stop crying louder & take the situation in his control. With respect on the professor who got stuck in this ruckus, I gave a look towards him and in return, he replied, "I am helpless." Vicky started slapping the other 2 girls & shouted to take the situation in his control by creating a sense of fear among the students and looked towards me.

I lost my senses after seeing Vicky slap those girls. Then, my IN ME was on the rage to conquer the situation in seconds. I picked the fire extinguisher in my right hand from the pillar beside me and dragged it back to my shoulder to attain force and hit on the ribs of Vicky (though my heart was shouting to hit on the head, but I didn't do that. Somewhere my mind dominated some moral senses in me). When Vicky was strongly hit on the ribs, other bad seeds came forward to defend Vicky by attacking me in all possible ways. Few bad seeds started throwing solid things on me they found in the surroundings. The fire extinguisher was still in my hands and I was surrounded by 11 Bad seeds. Vicky was at back of them, trying to recover from the hit with the support of other 3 bad seeds.

I opened the pin of the fire extinguisher and aimed at the faces of all eleven bad seeds who circled me. The extinguisher emptied after a minute and the eyes of all the eleven got disturbed, they were unable to open their eyes. I started hitting on their ribs, shoulders and backs with the emptied fire extinguisher. Three bad seeds who were holding Vicky at the back of these eleven, came forward to fight and started throwing flower pots & water filters on me. I took a steel plate of about 24-inch diameter, which was used to cover the water filter from the top and started hitting those 3 bad seeds on their faces, it resulted in breaking the teeth of one among them. In parallel, Vicky started running away from the location after witnessing all the ruckus. I started chasing Vicky by leaving behind all the 14 bad seeds. The entire campus was witnessing this. While chasing Vicky, I heard this from someone,

"Where did these rebels go? Here, Madan alone has started fighting with these bad seeds."

Vicky was getting clearly out of the way from the students in the campus as no one dared to stop him because of the panic created after the ruckus. Vicky fell from the stairs while he was trying to descend the stairs by skipping 3 stairs at a time. I reached to him and caught his half unbuttoned, opened shirt and hit hard on his teeth with my fist, resulting in injury to his lips and my wrist equally. I had to release his shirt because of the pain in my wrist. We both ran half a kilometre more. While chasing resulted in heavy breathlessness and unsteadiness, my ego was satisfied as the situation was under my control with Vicky before me, injured and in an attacked condition. I was then trying to stand steadily by reducing breathlessness and observing everything around me.

Vicky was trying to catch something beside him with the intention to attack me. I immediately became alert and hit him hard by grasping his back hair tightly and held his head to hit on his lips with my raised legs and this resulted in bleeding from his mouth. Meanwhile, the bad seeds reached to rescue Vicky from me and circled me again to attack but this time there was no fire extinguisher or any water filter near me. I observed the curtains on a glass door beside me and pulled the curtain hard from the stand. Then, I wrapped the curtain cloth on my hand and hit the glass door hard to break the glass. The glass broke in large, small pieces. With wrapped curtain, I picked a medium piece of the broken glass to defend myself from all those 14 bad seeds. They circled me and I started looking round the circle of the bad seeds surrounding me. The situation was like, the campus was witnessing the rage happening before them with a mixed thought that rebels were not there in the campus and of me alone attacking those bad seeds. On the other hand, the bad seeds tried their best to show their best impressions before Vicky by hitting me.

I was searching for a lead in the situation to attack the bad seeds surrounding me. Unexpectedly, I felt a hard hit on my back and neck with a sharp & hard material, resulting me to fall down on the floor in a tripping manner. My nose & tongue were badly injured. There was a slight cut on my tongue which made way for blood to ooze from my mouth and abrasion scratches on my nose made the way for burning sensation to occur on my nose. Fiercely, I turned around to find the one who hit me, it was Prashant, the stout guy among all in the bad seeds, who had hit me badly with a knuckle duster.

In a settled technique, I was controlling the circumstances till then, but after he attacked with his knuckle duster, I lost my temper and started attacking them violently. Within no time, I reacted by grasping a hair tuft of Prashant with my right hand & made his head bent till the level of his chest. I placed my left hand on his shoulder, my left foot on his thighs and climbed on him by placing my right knee on his shoulder, and started looking fiercely towards all the bad seeds surrounding me.

I was looking completely dominant by standing on knees on the shoulders of the toughest guy among all the bad seeds, and the surrounding crooks stepped back by looking at me in heavy breathlessness, mixed with anger & a fierce spark. Prashant was there, under my knees, trying to hurt me by making some movement, which made my anger to rise high. I held his head by placing it in between my palms, my left hand holding his jaw below his mouth & I grabbed his hair with a fitted grip and twisted his head, which injured him badly, resulting him to collapse on the ground. I made a move of football kick to his stomach & turned back to get the other two guys in my attacking zone. Six of the bad seeds started running away from me in fear, and one after another, all the bad seeds dispersed from the location. My breathlessness was not coming under control after this incident during fest inside the college campus. I sat down on the floor, resting beside a wall to make myself relaxed and bring my pulse rate under control. After a few minutes, it felt normal to me. The students surrounding me looked at me with fear and some looked at me with respect, but a large number of students came near me, also with those three girls & that one professor with whom the bad seeds misbehaved. They started thanking me by holding my hands; the girls started wishing me to get well soon from the injuries on my tongue, nose & hand.

It took fifteen minutes for me to come out from their gratitude and I settled the things around me after this incident, trying to search some peace in the surrounding air, but everywhere I saw were the faces smiling with gratitude. Every time, after such incidents, I used to search my rebels to share the sense of intensity in the incidents. But that day, my heart was scratching my brain to not think of Mrudhula, though she would know about the incident before evening or she may have known by that time. An interrogation session began in my 'IN ME', on her for not coming near me or even in my eyesight after this huge disturbance in the college fest. The complete campus was feeling thankful but how come she was not at all there? Though those many were thankful but I was not getting the happiness. I realized how good I felt when this woman was with me & how down I felt in her absence. Even the world surrounding me was happy because of me, but I didn't feel happiness.

Days passed, weeks passed, I was not getting any trace of Mrudhula in the campus. Gradually, the charge of my excitement was getting down and feelings of disappointment were increasing. In her absence,

*My **thoughts** running behind her,*

*Recollecting the glimpse of her **voice** from our past conversations.*

***My Heart** feeling unrest and I started seeing myself in her Flashing image, sparkling.*

***My Mind** sensing her absence.*

***My Eyes** which dreamt of her started searching for the ray of hope to see my mind's flashing image before me.*

*I couldn't imagine my **path** to reach the destiny without her.*

Fifteen days passed, on August 5th, 2005, it was our college founders' day. After our principal addressed the students in the event, the rebels started chitchatting, outside the examination cell in the campus, on the recent movie releases and imitated the mannerisms and styles from various movies.

Suddenly, Rihan said with excitement in a medium voice, "Hey, Madan, see there, it's your sister-in-law standing there," I didn't understand what he was trying to say & whom he was pointing towards, I gave a confused look to him and asked, "What are you trying to convey, I can't decode this, what happened?" "Look at that girl in a blue top, she is the younger sister of Mrudhula," said Rihan.

The lady in the blue top before us heard the conversation, turned towards me and started looking at me angrily. I was confused & totally clueless on how to handle this situation. I was looking towards Rihan, asking him of what had he done, "I think you have damaged the spider web in my heart now," Parallel to this, she (Mrudhula's sister, I didn't know her name) walked away from the place by keeping the same angry look at me.

My IN ME started worrying about the possible consequences in the relation with Mrudhula now. It had been fifteen days since I saw her & after that incident in the college, I didn't know what impact it might have made on her. At that moment, I didn't know what her sister felt and was going to convey. I was unable to think of the possible miscommunication which going to take place in my life, I couldn't vent out this feeling of hindrance, I somehow kept the things on stake with my overconfidence & ego. For my sake, I realized that I could handle any situation which was not close to my heart, *whatever be it; the damn violence, social issues, withstanding the belief on me in the campus, standing for the villages surrounding the college, local settlements, fistfights, safeguarding the old age homes, eradicating child labour in my adjacent world and a lot more.* The strain graph of my IN ME started rising & I couldn't vent the strain out by smoking, drinking or throwing things away, nor I could create a mesh. I started to hit hard on my chest with tightly closed fist, started hitting the heart, increased the pace on hitting, hitting, hitting, hitting by shouting and kicking on the wall with the front portion of my closed fist. I hit on the chest with a side portion of my wrist, I didn't feel any sense of pain on my wrist, this was how I vented out the feeling of hindrance from me. Usually, such situation came rarely, I guess this was the third time I was doing this. I could handle the things with my planning, my every thought came with basic planning only. I never plan to make the things planned, planning is integrated in my thoughts, each thought would have at least 3 sub plans to overcome the situation.

At 5:30 pm, college completed, I didn't know where was the house of Mrudhula & where she came from but I knew in which direction she walked home. I decided to meet her & apologize for what had happened today with her sister. Waiting on the lane where she walked home, after around fifteen minutes, I saw her after fifteen days at an approximate distance of fifteen meters. She saw me and continued walking without any eye contact. I was not having enough dare to walk towards her and start a conversation, my IN ME started kicking me which led my footsteps towards her diagonally and crossed her path. She started looking at me by stopping before me.

Mrudhula: What happened, why are you here? Is there any other mesh or fistfight here?

Me: No.

Mrudhula: Oh, are you going to create anything like that?

Me: (with slightly shivering words) Why are you thinking this?

Mrudhula: (in a confident and dominating tone) Then, how can I think of you or how can I look at you?

I was staring at her blankly without any dialogue.

Mrudhula: What was that mesh you created in the college on that day? How did you beat them alone, they were fifteen guys with the intention to harm you and you were alone with an overconfidence of attacking them, was that necessary for you?

Me: No, but they were trying to harass three girls and one professor, so I just tried to calm down the situation, but Vicky slapped the girl before me, so I couldn't control that.

Mrudhula: So, were you the only one in the fest? Why didn't others respond to that? Why did only you start to settle the things? Where were your other friends? Why only did you start? What if they injured you? You fell after being hit with a knuckle duster, what could have happened to you, you were alone and they were fifteen with an intention to injure you badly, was this necessary for you?

Me: I neither think about what others do, nor I could wait for someone to react and do some rescue. If I can, then I will and I am very confident to handle such situations. Also, it's not difficult nor I am new to handle such situations. I don't rely on someone coming to me and saving or handling the situation.

Mrudhula: (With her fierceness) Well, you controlled the situation, you suffered a lot, were injured too. However, did the girls or professor come with first aid to you? They just expressed their gratitude and left the place, but you were injured & took the pain, was this right?

Me: I don't do and even didn't do that by expecting something in return.

Mrudhula: Ok, it's up to you, why are you here?

Me: But how do you know all this, you were there on that day? Mrudhula: Why are you here?

Me: I want to apologise to you.

Mrudhula: Apologise? Why? What else you did?

Me: That blue top lady, is she your sister?

Mrudhula: Yes, she is Jhansi. What happened to her?

Me: No, nothing, didn't she say anything to you?

Mrudhula: No, she didn't, what happened?

Me: Nothing, nothing, everything is ok.

Mrudhula: Tell me what has happened, or I will ask her after reaching home and she will tell me.

Me: Some of our friends spoke something about our relationship before her and she left the place angrily after hearing that, I felt bad and today itself I came to know that you have a sister. Please excuse me & my friends.

Mrudhula: Please listen to me; mind it, ask your friends to be in their limits and this must not be repeated with anyone else.

Me: Ok, sorry.

She left from there then, I paused and stared at her walking, with many thoughts in my mind. That lane was so big that I got at least three minutes to see her walking; it was like a lady horse walking in the lane. If I needed to walk with her, I may have needed to take a cycle to match her walking speed and beauty in her walking.

I was relaxed after this conversation; the air in my thoughts was cleared and filled with joy by her concern for me. The stress of fifteen days had come down and the volcano in my heart settled calmly inside the room of joy. I giggled.

The next day there was a presentation from our college in Kailashgiri convention hall. This hilltop convention hall with a sea view with abundant greenery was my favourite & Lord Shiva & Parvathi statues on the top of the hill was the place where my soul felt relaxed.

There was a call from the auditorium stating to get ready with the presentation within fifteen minutes before your turn to present. I said, "Of course, I am ready with the presentation," to the coordinator. "Don't you revise the presentation at least once before presenting," were the words of a lady with a voice similar to Mrudhula's. I turned back to look who she was. It was Mrudhula looking at me dominatingly and stood confidently by folding her hands. "Hey, what are you doing here, good to see you, Mrudhula. I am feeling so happy that you are here," I said.

"Don't you do a quick revision before a presentation?" She asked with a mixed emotion of concern and anger. "I generally don't prepare for interviews and presentations because I commit to what I say and I say if I believe it logically, so no need of revision in presentations or preparations for interviews, whatever be the topic, if am confident I will conquer, else I won't step in."

"Is this not overconfidence in you?" She asked again.

"Hey look, you are looking at my confidence just for the second time and you're judging it as overconfidence, don't worry, there are a lot of incidents, situations that you may witness further, where I will not step in for small and simple things. I will make my IN for risky, complex things where I feel confident."

"Generally, I don't make things planned nor I think to achieve the situation completely, I just acknowledge the practical stuff and go ahead. I am never bothered about the gain in the situation. Rather than winning the situation, I prefer to excel in the situation." Meanwhile, I got the call from the auditorium stage regarding my presentation, I started moving ahead of Mrudhula, and I pulled my shirt in, folded its sleeves till elbows, and snatched the belt from Rihan and combed hair with my fingers. I paused for a while, turned back and looked towards Mrudhula with a funky body language and a funny face expression. With a smile, I asked her not to wish me 'all the best' because I don't believe in this stuff. "Now watch my show from here," I said and stepped on the stage.

All these frames happened in seconds after the announcement

and one more announcement was made, calling me to be present on the stage.

My presentation ended with great cheers and claps. During the presentation, the panel of judges appreciated me and after it shook hands with me by patting on my shoulders. They praised the way I presented without looking at the PPT, the way I owned the deliverance of the concept and the confidence in my debating points.

"Congratulations, Mr. Madan, you stole the show, I felt great while witnessing your presentation," She said with a good smile. "Thank you Miss Mrudhula, it's my honour to get your appreciation, I am feeling high after getting your appreciation here because it doesn't matter to get compared or if a talented person accepts the defeat, but it does if our loved ones appreciate us, this is totally an incomparable feeling of victory."

A group of classical dancers was coming towards us, I could see them, but Mrudhula couldn't see them as we stood opposite to each other. I was surprised to see a group of 5 dancers coming obediently. My facial expression was changing to that of more surprise with their distances nearing me. Mrudhula observed my change in expressions and turned back to see what had made me surprised. The group of ladies obediently greeted Mrudhula and stated, "Within fifteen minutes our program would begin, Madam, can you please get ready?"

Now, I was more confused and was looking at Mrudhula and asked,

"What's happening, who are they and what is the program scheduled in the next fifteen minutes?" Mrudhula dispersed with a smile, though that smile from her made me feel happy but did not make my confusion down. I tried to ask one of the girls in that group regarding the program and what Mrudhula was going to do and how she was linked with the team, but none of them turned back and left the place politely.

I followed the group of dancers with the signal of that smile from Mrudhula. There was actually one more cultural program scheduled at the top floor of the auditorium where we gave the presentation. I saw the board displaying 32ndAndhra Kuchupudi classical dance event, 'It is a statelevel competition, but what Mrudhula is doing here, is she a classical dancer or an event organiser or did she come to support someone in this event,' Many such unanswered questions were running across my mind.

The security stopped me at the entrance and asked for an entry pass to the event. "Please allow him inside," said a female voice. It was Divya, asking the security to allow me inside the event. I said a 'hi' to her and asked, "What is this, what are you all doing here, why Mrudhula is here, is she supporting someone or is she helping the organizers of this event?" She stopped my series of questions by showing her palm and said, "Mrudhula is one of the best Kuchupudi classical dancers, she is learning this art from class fifth and she is one of the best dancers in the state.' I stopped walking with her and looked at her with surprise, "Are you serious? I am not getting to how I should react and what more to ask you, is she performing now? Can we watch the performance?" I asked her, waiting for her reply.

'Mrudhula Krishna & her team is performing next, on *Ganesh sthothram*' was the announcement. I heard and looked towards Divya. I then moved fast from there into the auditorium with excitement to watch her dance and watch her appearance in that traditional dance costume. But, there was no vacant seat found in the auditorium and thus, I continued to stand in one corner. The team with Mrudhula as the lead, entered the stage, and the crowd in the auditorium started clapping, with smile on their lips and raised eyebrows. People in the auditorium were expecting to witness one of the finest performances. I was surprised and was feeling limitlessly happy, proud for the things happening before me.

This was completely unexpected and far beyond from my thoughts. Their performance started with the music and *namaskar* in a classical pose. Though I was not a listener of classical music; even for a minute, but the visuals before me, made my legs tightened to the floor and I started witnessing the wonder before me and around me. Her performance on stage was completely a new package of joyful love and the audience's expectations around me were making me feel overwhelmed.

Undoubtedly, it was the best moment of my life.

Cherishing the present, I never felt moments from my past and never imagined my future.

Her performance on stage was like that of a lady version of lord *Nataraja*; her fierce eyes, confident attitude, classical body language and perfection in her foot movements. Soft drinks came before me and were offered, I picked a glass without taking eyes off from her performance on stage. Observing the audience in my surroundings, I was completely filled with pride, joy, and respect for her and her divine performance continued for ten minutes. After the performance, the entire auditorium was clapping by giving a standing ovation.

It took nearly five minutes for her to come down from the stage after greeting, thanking all who were appreciating and congratulating her and her team for the performance. I silently stood aside the wall and enjoyed the moment by witnessing all those best wishes for her talent, it took more the twenty minutes for her to come out from the team.

She came to me with a smile on her face, I was looking at her smiling with a very pleased and gladdened demeanour, and we both were facing each other in the corridor of the auditorium. Apart from shy smiles, no conversation was taking place between us. "You were amazing, Mrudhula, your performance was outstanding, *you have a magic to attract people not only with your smile, but also with your beauty. For the first time, I am feeling your beauty after witnessing the talent in you. Though you are a beautiful girl, but I never fell for your beauty, I never thought of getting you in my life for the sake you are beautiful, now me and my heart have completely fallen for you with your charm."*

"Madan, shall I say to you something? *I know I am enough talented in my world; I feel good and satisfied, but I never felt proud of myself, but when it comes to you and the thought of thinking you, I completely feel proud and admire.."* "Wait, wait, wait....!" (I paused her)

"What made you say this?" I asked her.

"Your thought process, your maturity on social responsibility and if you remember our first conversation," She said *"It was like wow to listen to those intentions from people in this society, I would love to explore more about you."*

I never thought of exploring any Man, excluding my father, but you are the first man I thought of exploring and tried to spend time around you without your knowledge. After fistfights with those bad seeds in the campus, every day, I used to enquire about you and your well-being, you were missing me but my concern was around you. I started this enquiry from the moment you collected complete food from our stall in the fest. Divya went behind your friends to know what you are going to do with such huge quantity of food, she found a way to orphanage home which you were supporting by collecting funds and you were joining the children involved in child labour. The food which you collected was managed for their lunch, and dinner on that day. We kept that stall to gain some profit and have some experience in managing the planned investment, but with concern towards me, you changed the game completely and took my thoughts towards those children. With a proud feeling for you; I myself felt proud by donating some amount to that orphanage home on Wednesdays, every week. Your passion of taking care, providing good shelter, food to unknown children on the footpath is incomparable to the appreciations or claps which I got today. You may start loving me for what I am, but I started admiring you not for what you are, I started admiring for what you mean. Every life on this earth has a reason to come on earth and very few know, realize and act accordingly, you are one of those very few people.

After listening to her version, I was completely mute with heavy emotions inside me, "I have no words to say, I need some time Mrudhula," I said to her.

"I have some more words to complete," She said.

"Your intentions are good, but the approach you must have to achieve those intentions is not correct. You are lacking peace, don't try to be the master of all cards, you are involved in stopping child labour, stopping eve-teasing, stopping cruel intentions of the bad seeds in the campus, standing in support of the local villagers, leading your team of rebels, these many activities are making you engaged everywhere with incorrect approach. Try to cross-check your activities and start questioning yourself, are these giving you peace? If no is the reply, then how can you make peace in your surroundings without achieving peace within yourself. Also, are you about to complete the degree with a good percentage?"

Lub Dub

"I need some time to discuss this," I said to her and dispersed from there with very mixed thoughts in mind & pleasant emotions in heart. I, alone sat in our college canteen, with the same thoughts in mind, and was unable to conclude but couldn't deny her version for me. ***"Don't try to be the master of all cards"*** was the sentence that was running in my mind, my thoughts were going deeper and cross checking my approach of achieving the result in various activities. I still needed some discussion with Mrudhula on this before any conclusion. After almost one hour that I had spent in the canteen, I went to the ground, which was out of campus for playing volleyball with the rebels. Most of the rebels were thinking these days that I had lessened spending time with them.

In the coming month, we had exams of the final semester. I thought to spend some quality time in preparation to get good score in the final semester. One more thing I didn't reveal to Mrudhula yet was that I cleared 22 backlogs till my previous semester with 5 labs practical in it. My average aggregate percentage had increased, but this final semester exams were very crucial to maintain the scale and improve the percentage.

Before going to bed that night, my sister came to me and started asking, "What happened to you, since the last couple of weeks you are not looking normal, are you stable?"

"Yes, I am fine and completely good," I said. She returned to her room looking at me; she was unanswerable after listening to my words. I went to bed to sleep.

I tried to wake up gradually after hearing the morning music of '7 am' news on our television in the hall. The news headlines were disturbing my sleep and were creating a mood to wake up from the bed. As usual, I checked my Nokia 3310 mobile for any messages or calls. After my breakfast, as usual, I started towards college by thinking those words from Mrudhula yesterday. I called her to meet me at the college canteen to discuss. She said she was not coming to college that day, she had some work at home due to a marriage proposal for her elder sister, a gentleman & his family were coming to their house.

"That's a great news, Mrudhula, convey my best wishes to her & can you try to meet me today evening at Ram Mandir in your next lane?" I asked. "Okay, I will be there by 5pm" She said and shut the call.

I think she understood what could be our discussion on. When I was speaking with her on call, her voice modulation was something nice I felt, I decided to open my views with her to make the changes as we needed. I reached Ram Mandir by 4:55pm, the parking lot was full already, so I parked the bike on the roadside. Mrudhula came towards me by waving her hands with a shy smile. I asked her to come near me, with an action of welcoming her with my palms moving towards me.

I bought two ice creams and gave one to her. I opened the top covering wrapper of my *ice cream* and threw it on the road, which made her angry. She asked me to pick it up and throw it in the dustbin. I said, "*Just leave it, this is a road, not a park or a ground; that paper cover of ice cream would stick to some vehicle and move away, nothing will stay here on the road.*" "Why are you bothering about that ice cream paper cover, we came here to discuss something important which would have a positive impact on us from now," I said. She was not convinced with me on not picking up that ice cream paper cover, and went a few steps ahead onto the road and tried to pick it up by bending on the opposite side of the vehicles running. A *truck with high speed hit her in the fraction of seconds, she swept away from the road and fell 200 meters away from the hitting spot, it was a bloodshed across the road,* ***"My love lady in my heart stopped just in the span of one Lub dub of my heart."*** My mind was left completely blank and it was far from the belief of the frame that just happened before me. People around me started running towards her. I was still standing, my breath stopped at the moment when I saw her picking the ice cream paper cover and truck at high speed behind her just a second before it hit her. I was paused for a while & tried to inhale the left breath into me, no movement was streaming in me from my legs to eyes. I was far from believing the frame that just happened before me. What happened before me at this moment was completely brutal, my IN ME had been stopped completely. I stood still with the happenings and belief of the frame I saw. People started calling the ambulance, I slowly tried to regain my senses and came into this world from that pause, started walking towards her with a collapsed heart, wet eyes & shivering legs. The crowd around me was crying loudly after witnessing such a horrible, brutal incident on the road that happened in a fraction of seconds. Without any senses, I was still walking to reach her; my legs collapsed while walking, my knees collapsed to feet & I nonsensically started crawling. People around me started witnessing me walking on knees and tears rolling down my eyes. Loud screams of cry were heard everywhere, I went near, crawling with knees and saw the shattered face and hands of Mrudhula. Those last words of throwing the ice cream paper cover on the road with an anger on her face were gone and I walked a few steps on to the road to pick up the last frame of the communication we had between us. My words, which I said to her on picking the paper cover, ***"Just leave it, this is a road, not a park or a ground, that paper cover of ice cream will stick to some vehicle and move away, nothing will stay here on the road"*** was making my head rotate and it was still alive in my ears. I was unable to cry after seeing her without any movement.

Her Fierce eyes were now closed.

Dreams before my eyes were shattered.

Her running toes stopped before my unbalanced feet.

Heartbeat started hitting me
like crushing waves in a wild sea.

Her Aura started getting in me & in my thoughts.

I came back into the world of reality and tried to take a breath hardly to get the support of the social aura surrounding me. Tears rolling down my eyes were getting the message from the world around me to 'take care of people'. Lost time was the most precious time in this situation. I was trying to regain my senses by feeling her aura in me. I went near her, saw her, touched her hands and saw those bruises on her hands. I could never see a single cut or injury on her hand, but that day, because of me, her entire body was crushed in parts. I was not getting any part of her body to hold and cry for expressing the pain in me. I had never touched her before, even her fingers, now this was the first time I held her hands & legs (which were only available in parts after the truck crash). I saw her hand and the cuts on her hand, I started crying with *guilt, loss, and hurt.* I couldn't see her in such a condition. I had never imagined her face without a smile even in my thoughts. In the meantime, ambulance guys came to me, asked to leave her, and they were taking her from the location. I left her hand and saw that injured cut mark on her hand while leaving her hand for the last time.

I was seeing the hair on her hands

I was seeing those nails on her hands

I was seeing that colour on her hands, which she had applied to perform in yesterday's classical dance.

I was seeing those fingers of her hands

I was seeing those lines in her hands

I felt that first & final touch of her,

I left her hand completely and collapsed down on the road.

I started crying hard by beating myself on the road with a thought, 'She is no more.' I started cursing God by questioning him, scolding him, tried to beat him in the air surrounding me and people around me came to me and recognized that I could be someone who could tell her details, address and family members' contacts, but no one was trying to come near me and ask for details. The rebels reached the location by knowing this incident through some sources and held me, consoled me, and tried to control me by taking me in their arms. I was still in those thoughts of meeting her and discussing the best to be done from my side to have the fair relation among us. The situation was entirely different in reality here.

I was forcefully picked by all the rebels by them stating, "You can't handle or see this anymore, we will take care and we will balance things with her family." I was sent to my home forcefully. I was tied and guarded by 6 of the rebels and travelled through the path where our college came on the way. After seeing the college campus main gate, I burst into tears again, tried to come out of the vehicle by opening the doors in the middle of the road, but Rihan controlled me by pulling my hands, and not allowing me to open the doors of our Innova. I witnessed one body was going towards the cremation ground with a rally of people on the side of the road, this visual before me got my inner pitch high, I shouted loudly and started crying inside the vehicle. I couldn't see this happening to Mrudhula. I could not let her go like this. The driver got panicked after looking at me and stopped the vehicle immediately on the side of the road and turned back to control me. This time, Rihan was unable to control my pain from pulling the lock to open the door. I kicked Rihan out from the door and started running back to the incident location. All the six members started chasing to catch me, I started crying and collapsed on road after running for some distance, all my friends came to hug me and comfort me. They started crying along with me. I was in no way to get someone stop me to reach the incident location. Again, I started running back to the incident location. While running back, I reached to that rally where someone's body was being carried. I felt connected to the emotions of those family members in rally, who were unknown to me and started hugging them, crying with them and making them cry. At this point of time, I felt we were in the same line of emotion and pain for our loved ones. No one thinks of meeting someone in such situations, but I felt truly empathetic with them. I opened myself with them; I started crying and shared my pain by simultaneously crying with them,

I realized true love will not come in our happy times, nor with the best people we have, it will come in these final journeys and it can come with strangers also. I don't know and was not caring about what they were thinking after I shared my pain with them, they started to open up and started sharing their pain and constraints which they had. I was shocked to see them opening with me in sharing their pain, the rally got on hold now and people started witnessing us; we all were strangers who had started sharing pain with each other without knowing each other. Maybe, this was an unsaid emotion, which was more powerful than trust & belief.

I started running back to the incident location. My friends caught me and brought their vehicle. They made me sit inside and started taking me home. This time, I couldn't escape, nor they could handle me, but consoled me with high emotions and a lot of apologies. We reached home, my sister was alone at home and I don't know, from where my parents came. She understood something untoward had happened with me, everyone was crying and she saw me inside the vehicle. She started screaming loudly and ran towards the vehicle.

Thereafter, seeing me and my avatar, she reached towards me and held my hands. By pulling me out of the car, she asked "What happened, why are you like this?" I kept calm, 'How could I tell her, *she's one lady in my life whom I loved a lot from her first breath, and now how can I say to her that I lost one more lady and I was the reason of her last breath*." No one was ready to speak up; everyone was looking at each other. With her love and affection, I started crying by hugging her, *whatever be the attitude or strength the man has, in his downtimes only a woman can control him and console him, such a powerful gift God has given to a woman and to a man*. I started crying out loud, but was unable to say or communicate anything. She saw bloodstains on my shirt, pants and hands, "What are these bloodstains, what happened to you, what made you to have these stains on you?" She started shouting loudly and crying by holding my hair.

My mother came walking towards me by seeing the rebels outside the house and seeing her two children crying like anything made her run towards us and she started questioning, tensed,

"What happened?"

"Why Madan is like this?"

"What is this blood?"

"Why is his hair disturbed and blood is on his body?"

"Why are his eyes red?"

"Why is his shirt torn?"

"What are those scratches on his hands and elbow?"

"Where is your dad?"

"What made you come out and cry here?"

She shot all these questions quickly with tension and fear. This is what the mother's love is, no matter what happens to the world & what happens in the world, her concern for you is always there. No one had observed these changes in me, even I didn't see myself. I just realized after listening to her questions on how my avatar was, she didn't stop those questions. In this situation, how could have I said to her that,

You gave me life by giving birth and I lost my life by pushing Mrudhula towards death, how could have I handled my sister by saying, ***you are the lady in my life whom I love a lot from your first breath, now how can I say to you that I lost one more lady and became the reason of her last breath.*** Rihan came forward and kept his hand on my shoulder and started crying. I asked him, "Who were our guys there at the location and what happened?"

"Her parents had come to the location," He replied. My sister asked me, "What happened, whose parents, who is she?" Without replying anything, I went inside my room and started searching for the bike keys and realized the bike was at the location.

Hence, I asked Rihan to give his bike. I needed to go there. My mother stopped me by holding the collar of my shirt. I burst into tears before her, cried kneeling down before her. Rihan started saying everything that had happened.

My mother came near me and started crying loudly after listening to what had happened. She let me go there and said, "Keep calm and make yourself stable from the situation, I have a belief on you, go there, listen to your heart and reach her house to see and do everything what can be done for her." Her words filled the strength in my heart to stand before the pain and hurt. I started with my sister & friends, towards Mrudhula's house.

I thought of my sister and mother standing behind me in this situation and how they had boosted my morale to stand before the challenge of my life. I reached Mrudhula's house, I didn't know anyone there, thousands of people stood before her house. I saw both her sisters crying there, her younger sister too, towards whom Rihan once pointed. She came closer to me and asked, "How do you know this information, who told you about this?" I understood that none did know what had happened; they were just thinking this was a road accident. I was about to say what had happened to her and how. In the meantime, Rihan came and pulled me back to our group by understanding my version of further conversation that could spring up there and said to me, "No one knows what had happened, if you say everything, everyone would think about you and her, this society would not accept and would look at a narrow perspective" She is having a good impression amongst all, let it be. If you say what had happened now this could be a remark on her, and unknowingly, you would be the reason for her degradation in this situation.

"I understood your version, but how can we hide the truth, let the truth get revealed," I said. "Reveal it after a few months between the four walls of her house to her family members. If you start revealing now it will get distributed completely to all four corners of this society," He said.

"There is no mistake in what she did, right?" I asked.

"Please try to understand, Madan, this society will take the incident wrongly in the similar way they take the things with a narrow mind." He asserted. This stopped me and made me stand near her, she was completely wrapped and no one could see her.

Heart Quake

Three days had passed since her departure. My friends and family were trying to give a possible comfort to me, they were expecting me to come out of this situation in less time. There was no mistake in expecting this from their point of view, but the pain was in me and that couldn't have been understood or felt by any other in the globe around me. I went out for some reason and saw some papers, and covers thrown on the road by everyone. I started picking up every piece of paper, covers and threw them in the dustbin at the corner of our street. While returning back home, I saw a couple arguing among themselves for not witnessing a change in each other's behaviour and mindset as they needed. I saw that and listened to that for a while by standing at another corner. Tears started rolling down my eyes and I walked from there with a sad heart and a heavy weighted brain. My IN ME had stopped responding to me. Such memories were now coming across which made me put myself into the past with Mrudhula. I remembered those quotes from my childhood, when we used to go to the temple and listen to some preaching's, '*I can't count my time, even if I have my own watch and I may be the owner of my watch, but not of the time in that.*'

I was trying to connect a call to Rihan to know what happened in Mrudhula's house and when it could be the best time to talk with them and let them know what had really happened. Rihan was out of coverage area.

Life brought her to me like an elixir and took her away from me like poison. Many memories were linked with languageless intentions in me. People around me couldn't get them and I was not intending them to get it too. Everyone around me was making their best efforts to bring me out of this and no one around me tried to share any information related to the happenings in Mrudhula's house. I was unable to face her parents due to guilt and was not revealing the truth to them. Situations dominated me and played with me; situations made my mouth shut in the name of her respect.

In the name of her respect, everyone was trying to bring me out from the pain without knowing my actual pain. This was creating more discomfort to me. I thought to meet Divya, at least she could understand my pain as she was the one who knew the things better. But, I was not ready to call her to meet at some location. With a heavy heart, I kept walking with these entire conclusion- less confusions.

A group of some classical dancers was going inside a classical dance coaching centre. I felt relieved from those connections of language-less intentions in me. I sat on someone's bike under a banyan-like tree which was opposite to that coaching centre and looked at that coaching centre and the people in that coaching centre till evening. I couldn't make my move from that location because my language-less intentions were connected from those classical dance visuals in the coaching centre to Mrudhula' s performance on stage. The clock nearly tick-tock 08:00 pm, my legs & heart were still not moving from that location. I changed my seating from the bike to a bench below a tree. Someone came near me and asked, "Why are you crying, gentleman. What happened?" I said nothing and he went away with an unanswered facial expression. I realized that my outer appearance was also crying along with my inner appearance.

When our heart cries, we do not notice what our eyes are performing until and unless someone comes and notifies us.

The dance class got closed. It was around 09:30 pm at night, my friends and family members started searching for me because I left my mobile at home and came out just by seeing papers and covers on the road. I had just started walking after picking them and I had finally reached near that dance class. At that moment, I was not in the mood to go to home and face them back with their unanswered faces and language-less intentions. I was not feeling comfortable because of not knowing anything about Mrudhula and this wound was still in the flesh and I knew it would remain for a long time. My thoughts were not keeping my heart and legs settled. I was not searching for the medicine or was not feeling to think of the medicine for this wound too.

I kept walking by opening my five out of six shirt buttons. The cool breeze was hitting directly on my chest, but was not making any impact on my skin as the inner heart was completely heavy.

I was walking heavy footed, my heart was heavy, and my Mind was filled with the thoughts of Mrudhula.

My legs were not in a synchrony with my heart and mind because my mind was with Mrudhula, and where was Mrudhula? She was nowhere now. The meek voice tried to rise from my IN ME.

I reached the cremation ground with this confusing conversation in my IN ME and asked the man present there, "Where is Mrudhula?" He gave a weird look by communicating, "Who's she?" I asked again, "Where is Mrudhula?"

"Who's she? Many come here daily after ending their stories, many come in from that IN gate and get permanent exit pass from this world of sin."

Everyone comes here to reveal and relax their responsibilities. Everyone comes here and realize the fact of life.

Everyone comes here with loaded shoulders and return with loaded hearts.

Everyone comes here with a belief on love and get back with disbelief on life.

Everyone comes here with fear.

Everyone comes and realize here.

Everyone comes here with selfishness and return with reality.

Everyone will take many routes in entire life but all will take this final route.

Many come here in the end but I along with

Lord Shiva will be here.

I kept pause and was touched with a little relaxation after listening to his words and his intense confidence. I stood there with hope in my soul. I think he understood my pain and came near me. Keeping a hand on my shoulder, he asked, "What happened? Why are you here now, what is that pain which led you here at this time, let me know how can I support you."

I started explaining to him; all that happened, slowly, and presented myself before him with my current situation. He made me sit beside him in the cremation ground and asked me to look around for next five minutes, "You would get the solution of hope from your heart, there are many reasons for your heart to get the solution of hope from this place, let me know what made you relaxed, then I will speak to you," He said.

Darkness was everywhere, but those burning bodies only gave the flame of light.

Ashes everywhere, but warmness in the ash was giving the fragrance.

Skulls everywhere, but the reality of life was manifested from those ever-smiling skulls.

Silence everywhere, but a river flowing nearby was like the weapon to fight with situations.

Distress everywhere, but Lord Shiva's statue on a hill beside was like opening arms to hug me.

He came near me and asked, "What if your Mrudhula came back to you?" I don't know why I kept quiet and asked him, "Please tell me, where is she here, where were her last rituals conducted?"

He raised his hand by pointing his finger towards the river and said, "That heap beside the big stone is hers." Tears rolled down my eyes after seeing that heap of ash, my heart was still feeling I could be able to see her wrapped body which was my last image of hers, but I wasn't able to realize that everyone would be in this form only eventually. I started walking towards her ash beside the rock stone. My tears were increasing and the darkness due to tiredness covered my eyes along with the tears.

I took some ash in my hand and got that feel of holding her. All our conversations and visual frames started flashing in front of my eyes. I felt very much comfortable and relaxed after holding that ash. The tiredness in my body was increasing to make me fall on her ash. I collapsed on that heap of ash. Now, my body was directly in contact with her ash. I was feeling more comfortable after collapsing on her ash, there; continuously feeling better, my comfort levels started increasing.

This made me do the same for the next twenty days; daily roaming on our street and neighbouring streets, picking up the waste papers, clothes and wrappers and dumping them in our local municipal dustbins. I walked towards the classical dance institute, sat under the tree for hours and reached the cremation ground, slept in that place where Mrudhula's last rituals happened. Depression in my heart was not getting down and memories in my mind were getting stronger. This daily routine of mine made all my near and dear ones worried for me. My parents started to explore some possible ways to get me out from this daily routine, my friends were not uttering words in this situation; they all were running behind me to take care of me and look over my daily activities.

Those were the days, passed with rough and raw versions of life. My sister one day came to me and said, "You are good, you are genius, you are independent, you can do what you like, you may not be that path and hope for many people, but definitely, you are that ray of hope for a small group of people and I am one in that small group of people, you are our courage, your wellness is our wellness, you smile is our happiness, and your success is our pride."

"Stop all this, why are you saying all this to me?" I said.

"Your exams are approaching, you cleared all your supplementary exams, now you are having only the final semester exams. Can we expect you to clear these exams and do the things positively or else shall we skip this semester exam and wait for one more year?" she asked.

I thought for a while and said, "Don't worry I will do well and I can do well without preparation as well. I just need a review session before the day of the exam."

My sister was the one who brought me bit by bit out of my daily routine which was inherent from the last twenty days. She took me to the salon and made me sit before the mirror, asking me, "Is this ok?"

"Yes, this is ok, don't try to do more changes, let me be like this. I am feeling comfortable enough with this beard and long unshaped hair, you just need my final semester exams to get cleared and that will be done, don't worry and focus on yourself," I said this in a harsh tone and a rough look. I started walking out of the salon without caring what she thought or what the surrounding world was staring onto. I knew this was wrong but I had no other option to save my comfort.

My routine continued with searching books, avoiding eye contacts and skipping those roads which led me to this situation. This continued for the next fifteen days. After completing the exams, my parents came to me and kept a proposal in front of me to move out from Vizag for some days to get some fresh air and new thoughts to continue. I shouted at them with the same discomfort and shut the door hardly on their faces. This time, I didn't think this was wrong.

I felt like people were just forcing their ideas on me because I listened to them once. Everyone was coming to me and was keeping their demands before me to fulfil. This thought made my ego to have a 'thandav' in my IN ME. This made me walk towards the old road of life and I reached the incident spot, sat there on the road where that ice cream cover paper fell down & where a truck had hit Mrudhula.

Despite huge traffic on the road, I went and sat on that road with that intention coming out of my anger. I just wanted to let the truck come to me again and hit me hard or hit me badly. I didn't care, I owned this place now. I owned this road which took my Mrudhula away from me. I wanted to see how would someone come to me and take me away without returning my Mrudhula back to me.

Rihan and Divya were visiting the incident location regularly to get my traces whenever I was stuck up in comfort from her heap of ash in the cremation ground. Today, after seeing me sitting on the road, Rihan came towards me running to catch me, lifted me up and tried to hold me in a hurry. I shouted loudly on Rihan and asked him to get away, "Don't try to disturb my comfort zone by doing what I don't like." Rihan stepped back. I was madly sitting on the road, the traffic got halted with continuous horns, but no one came near me after I warned Rihan. After a few minutes, Rihan retried to clear the road by lifting me from there. He failed again to do that. Few minutes had passed and the traffic had increased. Police got the information of a traffic disturbance and arrived at the location and tried to make me go away. I started shouting at them loudly. They were not ready to understand my pain or comfort, as my acts were creating disturbance socially. They started to handle me roughly, tried to lift me up by catching my shoulders, I started kicking them. Rihan requested the police to leave me. After few minutes, they beat me with their *lathis* and shifted me to a nearby police station on Vizag beach road which was the college's nearby police station. The staff at this police station knew me well and they were aware of my past activities, as the station was near to my college. They tried to counsel me to bring me out from the current phase. I felt tired and slept in the police station.

After a little nap, I found myself in the police cell. I don't know when they shifted me and I saw my friends and parents discussing something with the police staff about my activities after the incident. They kept me inside the cell for two more days as per the request of my father. They couldn't hold me for more than 2 days without any crime. Thus, they took me in custody for two days looking over my condition as a request made by my father.

My father came after two days and discussed with the duty in charge of the police station, and this went on for other thirty minutes. One constable came to my cell and opened the door of the cell and asked me to come out. The duty in charge of the police station and the sub- inspector, Mr. Vijay, asked me to attend one more counselling session. They took me out for a counselling session which continued for three hours. After the session, those people who did my counselling gave a feedback that I was not ready enough to accept the versions in counselling. On the contrary, "I started counselling them in the session" is what they said. Mr. Vijay came to my father and told him,

"Everything went well, now you can take him home and do as per our plan." I didn't understand why Mr. Vijay told a lie to my father that everything in the counselling went well, why he didn't say what the counselling officers had conveyed to him? Maybe to come out or relieve my pain from their regular normal duties or to get rid of the unnecessary obligations. They told that lie and let me out, but one unanswered question started haunting me, "What is that plan which he told my father about, what can they do now?"

After three days, one evening, my father came to me and asked me to go to Delhi for a few days and stay in Sharma Uncle's house till I got a relief or change in mindset. I listened to this and came out of that discussion silently, without any reply. My father tried to force me to follow his decision, but I didn't show any interest to spend a second with him during this discussion. He didn't force me much to listen, but the thought of moving out from the city started in my mind with a mixed response. 'Visakhapatnam, this is my city which hugs me every-time I am down, this is the city which gives me wings to spread when I am high"

Now, how can I have a thought of settling myself by leaving my city when I am down again? I thought not to move anywhere to get myself okay, because only a mother's hug can give the warm motivation when we are down than any other woman's hug. Visakhapatnam was like a mother to me which gave me everything I needed and desired.

The next morning, my sister came to me again and sat beside me. She kept looking at the things in the room and started arranging the cupboard in my room. She had been keeping the things in my room in their respective places, where all my clothes were kept unevenly and haphazardly most of the time. She started keeping all my clothes in order without uttering a single word. I looked around after a while, asking her, "What are you doing? Why are you, housekeeping my room, why are you keeping the things properly in my room?" I asked.

"I couldn't keep you and your thoughts properly, at least, let me keep your things in a proper order. Maybe these visuals around you changes your thoughts," She said this with utmost emotions and tears in her eyes. This made me come down to her and I asked, "What happened, why are you like this?" She pushed me back and said,

"Don't you understand why am I like this, why everyone in our house is like this? Why are your friends roaming on roads when you are not at home?" I kept quiet and said, "Yes, I can understand, but please leave me alone for some days. It would take good time for me to change my comfort world and come into your comfort world, I really need some time to make things normal. The women in my life are just mummy, you and Mrudhula. All three of you are most precious to me and I have lost her now. Please give me some more time to change my comfort zone. All you people are thinking I am sad or depressed, yes, I am sad and depressed, but I am currently comfortable in this zone only. So, I am requesting every one of you to not disturb my comfort zone, else I might go to more degraded comforts," After listening to this, she came to me hugged me and started crying aloud.

I knelt towards her and settled her from the emotional ride between us. "Okay, I have understood your love, what are you expecting me to do, what makes you happy, what should I do? I have lost one precious woman in my life and I am unable to come out from that, but, at least, let me make the other two women of my life feel better and happy. Tell me, what I must do now, come on, order me," I said this confidently to raise her morale and make her feel good. She repeated what my father had said yesterday, "Please go to Sharma Uncle's house in Delhi and stay there for some days. There will not be any disturbance in your comfort zone and we would feel enough confidence on your wellbeing. Your mental thoughts can have some change where you will get some fresh visuals before you with new people around you."

Though I had mixed intentions of leaving Visakhapatnam and moving out from here, I kept quiet before her, and obeyed her version. I told her, "This acceptance is only to make you feel good, you are one of my precious women."

She conveyed the same to my father and the arrangements were made in 3 days for my stay and travel. Then, I got some clear picture that this could have been the plan between my father and Mr. Vijay, the duty in charge of the police station, on that day. I took off from Vizag airport to land at the Delhi airport after three days of all the commitments with my sister. Sharma uncle with his driver came to receive me at the airport. His driver took my luggage and settled it in the corner of the vehicle, and we fastened the seat belts and rode to his home. Sharma uncle showed me the India gate and the Parliament House on the way with some photos clicked by him. I understood he was trying his best to give me a good level of comfort and make me normal. I was just obeying and walking with him calmly. Till then, he didn't try to create any disturbance in my comfort zone and I didn't have any problem with his comfort zone.

The difference I realized was that Sharma Uncle was trying to create a comfort zone without much forceful mental rub on me than my family, probably due to the difference in relations or maybe the belongingness of my family members created a sort of dominance on me and new interaction with Sharma Uncle made some gap between us, giving us the best space. This was some change I felt as my father had said that going out and taking fresh air would give me the best way to come out.

Torch Bearer

Sharma uncle was a native of Visakhapatnam, and was currently working in the Office of Ministry of Home Affairs in Delhi. He has been my father's good friend since their childhood periods and was a good family friend of ours. Mrs. Sharma was working in human rights commission and they had two sons settled out of India (USA & London). I remembered connecting to all his family members, because we used to plan family trips in summer vacations during our school days.

Meanwhile, we reached his home and Sharma uncle offered me his room and asked his driver to keep the luggage in my room. Aunty greeted me with a warm smile and said, "I have prepared dinner for all of us, let us all have dinner together once you get ready here." I started walking into my room and rang a call to my parents to convey them about my happenings and commuting to the place. My sister grabbed the phone and started asking about my wellbeing there, I could sense her love and concern for me from her voice, the feeling of missing her started in me. I wanted to see her and share something with her and wanted to vent out some pain from me. I realized she is the only lady of my age group who could understand me better with positive love and concerned care towards me. But on her word only, I went there to make her feel good and happy. I kept quiet and replied accordingly, and shut the call.

Ten days had passed there in Sharma Uncle's house.

I was feeling a little comfort there due to the 'outer' bond between us, they were being reserved with me and were trying to accept everything that I felt and what I did. Every time, there was some or the other home guards standing out of his home as security, a feeling of being gentle before them arose. I thought of exploring some places out in Delhi. The clock ticked 10:30 pm. I conveyed to Sharma uncle that I wanted to go out and stay out for some quality time. I went out of home and took a metro which usually runs till 11:00 pm. I went on roaming like anything since no one knew me there, no one knew my past, and no one bothered about my identity. All that was not bringing my real version out.

I saw on one footpath there were some people below the poverty line and few beggars sleeping there. I went near them and started thinking of them and their lives; how those people were surviving there and what could be their daily routines with so much of intense cold in the winters, how they were able to sleep there, making their way. I was completely lost in these thoughts and sat on a stool which was between them on the footpath where they were sleeping.

A group of girls with decorated faces and shining dresses came on that footpath and stood fifty meters away from me. I didn't give much attention to them and continued on my thoughts of those beggars sleeping on footpaths. I thought to bring some blankets the next day along with me again when I strolled around there. The gala of this group of decorated ladies was increasing from around 10 women and the moment it started really increasing, I looked towards them with a question mark in my mind that who were those women and what were they doing there at that time with so much of decoration on them. After a while, I saw a few men walking on that side. It was like something interesting was going to happen there. With a bit of excitement for those happenings in the new city, I decided to remain as a witness to the happenings there. I had never seen such activities in Visakhapatnam. In Delhi, a new activity was taking place before me.

Few men who came towards this group of women were discussing with some of them and other women were looking in all empty directions. I was sensing something in my mind, but having all those visuals before me, I couldn't trigger what exactly was happening there. A few ladies walked with those few men after some discussion and other ladies who remained continued looking in the empty directions. It took fifteen minutes again to clear the group of decorated ladies before me, going with different men. Two more ladies remained from that group on the footpath and they seemed to discuss something amongst themselves.

I started walking from there as it was 12:15am already, maybe uncle and aunt would have been worried due to my absence at home till that time. Also, I had some fear by virtue of their positions and amount of security outside their home, those security guys could have found where I was or they might have known about this activity because I was new to this city.

I was walking to Sharma uncle's home with some random picture in my IN ME, but my IN ME was not in a state to conclude what exactly that activity could be. I reached Sharma uncle's home without any conclusion in my thoughts and I decided to go there daily and to look what was that entire episode happening.

Next day, again, my IN ME drove my legs to the same location at the same time; again, the same story repeated like yesterday, after a while again, two ladies remained. At last, I observed those two ladies. I could get some rough idea of their faces from yesterday; one lady was new whom I didn't look at yesterday and one lady was the same, one of those two remaining ladies of the previous day. I started walking from there as the time had struck 12:30 am. That day, it took fifteen minutes more to settle the happening, and I almost concluded that this was some illegal activity between men and women; maybe some extramarital affairs or some sort of brothel house activities at midnight. I reached home with a conclusion which could have been almost near to the reality.

This continued daily for the next 3 nights. So, after five nights of my daily visiting and witnessing, I observed there was a lady in common from all the five nights who remained back with another new lady daily. I didn't know what could have been the reason. In the middle of those five nights, on the third night, I tried to gather the courage in my IN ME to reach her and ask what was happening there and why she was waiting there at last, after the group was cleared. But, I didn't perform this stunt-like action before her and my courage gathered was not enough.

Then, by that time, that lady had started looking at me and walked towards me. I was thinking of the happenings and doubts about her in my IN ME, but the visuals before me contrasted to my thoughts. I tried to speak to her, but didn't because of not having been able to gather enough courage.

Then, I observed she was coming to me and she would reach me in the few seconds. My IN ME was saying to run away and escape from there, but my legs were steadily stuck to the ground and eyes were confidently looking at her, though my IN ME was shivering with a lack of generating courage.

She reached near and made an eye contact with a reckless face expression and questioned me with her eyes by raising her eyebrows. Without any conversation between us, I stood mute without an expression and a voice before her. She started looking into my eyes and came near me, turned around to me and re-questioned in the same way by raising her eyebrows. I kept continuing the same mute expression and with no voice. She sat on that stool on which I daily sat. She broke that few second of silence and asked, "Are you new?" I continued the same silence. "Where are you from and why are you here?" She asked. I walked from there without replying anything and reached Sharma uncle's home and without much thought, I slept off.

Next day, I reached the same place and the same story happened; this time again, she came to me and our conversation got initiated as,

She: What is your problem, why do you come here daily?

Me: (not showing much interest to talk) Nothing.

She: Why do you come here daily? What are you doing?

Me: I am new to this city and you don't need to know more than this.

She: Alright, why are you here daily, what do you need?

Me: (I thought she would get angry with my reply, but she was trying to continue the conversation) Nothing like that.

She: Don't worry, I have been watching you here from last one week, either you need something from us or you are meshed up with many doubts in you.

Me: Nothing like that.

She: Okay, it's up to you then. In this case, I don't want to see you again, here, tomorrow.

Me: It's nothing. How does it matter to you if I am here tomorrow?

She: Ok, I can understand, you are facing some disturbance inside you. Don't worry, everything will be settled soon in your life.

Me: What are you talking about and how can you say that without knowing anything?

She: I said what I thought and by what I understood.

Me: But who are you and what are you doing here with all these ladies daily, and why daily one different lady remains with you and what happens then?

She took the stool and threw it a little far away, and asked me to come and sit beside her. I again kept mute and continued standing before her. She tried to give me some comfort and said, "Don't worry, you can sit here, let's have some conversation to clear the air from our minds, once the air in our minds gets cleared, then we can decide whether to discuss or disperse." I felt this was something practical and problem-less version of her. I sat beside her to start the conversation and clear the air between us, her way of giving me comfort without disturbing my already-persisting comfort made me sit beside her without any sort of hesitation and further doubts.

She: You look much depressed from the inside, what happened? Why are you trying to explore the unknown outer world?

Me: How do you know? You are saying an almost similar version of me.

She: I am a Prostitute, life has shown me much depth, I can understand in which state people are, and how they feel.

Me: Yes, I understood that you are a prostitute, but I didn't come to a conclusion without confirming and knowing the facts. Also I feel you are elevating more of yourself.

She: Don't worry, you will know or realize it in our conversation gradually, I can predict any person's state of mind by looking at their facial expressions and body language.

Me: I think this is something nice and a good self-elevation, so stop saying about me and try to say about someone who is coming in our vision right now.

She: Why do you worry about revealing yourself, who can come here now in the dead of the night? Let us meet tomorrow in the day at any location as per your wish and let's have some session of exploring the people's state of mind. Cool?

I said, "Ok, let us meet tomorrow at 3:30 pm at Madina cafe near Delhi railway station," I stopped this conversation and dispersed. I started walking to reach Sharma uncle's house and was thinking of my changed state after gathering the courage to challenge her boldly.

Next day, when it was 3:30pm, I stood waiting near Madina café. I didn't know how I would meet her; she was a prostitute and we had conversation only once. I was thinking of myself on how I had started trusting her with a single conversation. Soon, my IN ME jumped up and started dominating by saying, though she was a prostitute, there was some different kind of honesty in her which we never expect, she didn't discuss anything related to money or any other stuff related to prostitution, nor had intentions to cheat, moreover she didn't select a location for me, she had left the choice to me.

"Hi hero," A voice came from my back. I remembered that we didn't even know each other's name and we were there just with a strange belief. She was walking towards me, came near and smiling asked, "What's your name or what can I call you?" "I am Madan, what about you?" I asked.

"Malini," She said. "Oh, nice meeting you, Malini. I was thinking of what belief has made me come here to meet you, we didn't even know each other's name and we decided to meet with some strange belief at our hindsight, I was actually rethinking my idea of meeting you, if it was right or wrong."

"Don't worry, Mr. Madan. You may not think of continuing this friendship with a prostitute, but I had thought of everything, yesterday, before finishing our conversation," She said.

"Can you please stop mentioning yourself as a prostitute, I am neither mature enough nor comfortable of imagining you like that." "Don't worry, Madan, as you like," She said and we selected a table in the café to have a seat and ordered some stuff to eat, and she started the conversation, saying, "What shall we discuss now? What do you need to know?"

Me: You are straight-forward, Malini. Get directly into the topic.

She: My version is not like this with everyone, Madan. Though I have explored physically with others, but mentally I am reserved, very few know that my name is Malini. Rest of the world knows me as Maaya.

Me: Okay, why is there such trust on me, what made you reveal the things to me without knowing anything about me?

She: What made you come here, even without knowing my name? I had only tried knowing your state of mind and honesty in your pain state and made a move towards you.

Me: I still could not believe that you can know the state of mind of the people around you; of course, you came near to me having the similar state of mind, so I didn't have any option or a chance to cut on your version. Can you brief me with some examples of how you explore or know the state of mind of someone around us?

She: Let me tell you how we can predict. See that person with the yellow t-shirt, who is walking with his face upwards and has little widened broad legs. But he has bit downed shoulders; he is carrying the burden of a big responsibility which he is unable to settle for a good long time, this has changed him mentally and automatically or unknowingly, has changed his physical appearance. You can follow him and observe him for a while to get a clear picture, he performs every job with a smile-less face and leaves the work without completing or closing it.

Me: I think you are right. After your explanation, even I am feeling the same. No need to follow him. Can you describe some more people?

She: Okay, look at that person in the red shirt walking hurriedly, as if wanting to catch something, with an excited face expression. Observe him for a while, he usually tries to get something but couldn't achieve it at last, he is a sort of dissatisfied soul with many limitations.

While she was saying this, I started following him; I was chasing him without letting him know. I was following him; he was trying to catch a bus and was searching for a bus. After a few minutes, he came to know it had departed from the stand. I didn't stop following him, he was trying to buy a water bottle from a shop, there were many mineral water bottles in the shop, but he was searching for a branded mineral water bottle. Though he intended for a mineral water bottle, he was not settled with the available options because of his limitations. I came back to her and said, "What you said was not exactly the same, but yes, almost similar."

She: Maybe that's due to the difference between the

understanding of my perception & that from your perception in looking at the things.

Me: Ok, I accept this, but sensing their state of mind with their body languages, couldn't be accurate.

She: Look at that lady wearing cream-colored top, she is breathing heavily with a tight face and is forwarding her footsteps bit forcefully than normal. She has a good amount of insecurity in her, this made her to be dominant in appearance to this outer world. Generally, women with insecurities do not try to be dominant, but she is breathing a bit faster than normal and her body language also is a bit faster, she is creating an impression with her aura that she is not that easy to be tackled by anyone.

I was surprised by her analysis of those persons. I also realized how much depth life had taught her which brought all this to her, and expressed the same to her. She just smiled and said, "**Karma, Dharma and Time** are three immortals in this world, never think beyond these three and never try to fly above these three."

She: I saw you for five days, continuously, with the same intensity of depression. Though I don't know the reason and can't conclude without listening to your version, I thought to get you at least a little out of your depression because you are a genuine soul in this selfish world.

Not that she was speaking something similar to my situation, but she was saying something beyond my experiences, which made me silent and I continued listening to her. At that moment, all my fears and doubts were washed away because I could sense a pain from her words and honesty in her intentions. Though she was a prostitute, I felt much better with her than being with all the selfish people around me and the interest of knowing about her initiated in me. But I thought this interest might spoil the understanding between us. I started to think while accepting and recollecting my sister's words she had said to me as my family sent me out of Visakhapatnam, "New persons and new places may bring out some new experiences for you which would help you to come out of this phase in life."

Breaking my thoughts, Malini said, "Okay Madan, I need to leave, I have some work, Bye". I asked her, "Is coming to that footpath daily at night the only option to meet you or you have any contact or email id, to communicate?"

"Let's meet here tomorrow at the same time as today's," and she left. I sat there for some more time and started thinking of some versions which I had come across in life after Mrudhula's incident. Starting from sharing the pain with those unknown people, when my friends were bringing me back from the incident's location, when I witnessed a last journey and jumped from the vehicle and ran to them; sharing that sort of pain in that last journey of some person on the road. And, that night conversation with the man on the cremation ground and now with Malini; on three immortal things of Karma, Dharma and Time. I couldn't connect all these experiences but something was being cooked inside my heart, which was not in a clear shape.

Keeping all this in mind, I started walking from the café and reached the metro to explore some sightseeing locations in Delhi. I reached the parliament, INDIA gate again and I had started to love spending some good time having a look on the tourists at INDIA gate, I patiently tried to observe unknown languages and tried to guess their state of mind as how Malini had predicted today. In most of the cases, the results came out wrong, my predictions didn't match their following acts. Still, I didn't give up as this was the first try of this new, interesting and useful concept. I ate some junk food at INDIA gate, and seeing the guarding police and army home guards, I felt proud, ***"Yes, this is My Country, This is my responsibility, These are my people and anything we all do in this country is for the collective betterment for all of us."***

I reached Sharma uncle's house by 9:00 pm and had some chit chat with uncle and aunt. They worked in respectable positions in serving the country, I showed the same respect towards them and conveyed them what I thought at INDIA gate, and also told them that till now without many reasons, I had loved Visakhapatnam very much, but after exploring Delhi and spending time at INDIA gate, that proud feeling of Being INDIAN had raised to the peak in my heart. They felt happy and shared some of their great experiences in the duration of their service too.

Next day, at 3:30 pm, I reached Madina café and stood waiting for Malini again. She came there after ten minutes and asked about my wellbeing and how did I pass time the previous day. She also asked me, why I didn't go to the footpath like I used to, daily. I shared that proud feeling which I experienced at INDIA gate the previous day and how I gained some confidence after the conversation with uncle and aunt that helped me sleep better after many weeks.

She: Well, what happened, what made you depressed for these many weeks or months, can I know that, Madan?

I started conveying to her; what had happened and how it all started, and the consequent phase of my Heart Quake I had undergone.

She: (after listening to everything) Sorry Madan, this is something not good which happened in the tragedy between you and Mrudhula, but there is definitely a reason for all the happenings we come across in our lives.

Me: I don't try to think about all this because such stuff is only useful to self-motivate ourselves.

She: Don't worry, I respect and accept your version, but let me tell you something which I believe and the next perception is up to you.

"We are just souls travelling in this universe, we have this physical appearance with gender, race, body, language, nationality; but everything is very much temporary.

Physically, we are complete strangers, but in our Soul travel, we are well connected. Before ten days, we were

complete strangers, but now we have a very good relation and understanding.

In part of this soul travel, our two souls have a good relationship based on our Karma.

Your soul knows my soul from our previous lives and is connected to it, this is one reason we are in a situation to discuss.

My soul has now enlightened your soul, which is that balance of Karma between our souls getting nullified; in this soul travel at some previous point, your soul

enlightened my soul which is getting nullified now.

Mrudhula was one soul which had only a limited Karma left with your soul and it got nullified for this life and

travelled ahead to nullify the balance Karma with other souls. Same is with your Parents, relations, and friends and with me even; we are just nullifying the balance Karma in our Soul travel.

Everything we do is interlinked with another activity. We physically may not know what, when, why, where and how these souls get connected, but our soul

recognizes the opposite soul and comes into interaction like how we did. Don't you think our relationship is strange and Soul travel is the reason for this?

In conclusion to this, what I would assure and convey you is, Mrudhula's soul travel with Madan's Soul does not have a beginning nor end with this life, her further Soul travel will join you; may be as your daughter or saviour or some other stranger soul like me.

Don't feel that nullifying Karma in this life will not get you another chance to meet the soul in the next life; it purely depends on what interaction happened between those souls in this life."

This version of Soul travel from her made me dumbstruck completely but convinced me up to some extent. Though this concept was new to me, it was understandable in my thoughts and it connected those unconnected dots, which I had thought about the previous day; those three incidents.

Breaking my thoughts, she said, "Hey Madan, did I say anything which hurt you or is out of your belief range? If so, just ignore what I said. I am not here to convince you, I just shared what I firmly believed in, also I feel this is my part in your life; maybe for this clarification your soul has travelled to Delhi where my soul is."

"What you are saying is logically correct and is in my belief range, but I need some good time to take it and digest in me, if I complete digesting it in my IN ME then my IN ME starts making it as a thought process for my further life. The relaxation point in your entire conversation is that our souls are not new and this is not the last chance, I have a chance to meet Mrudhula' s soul further in my soul travel," I said.

"Yes Madan, but as I just said, you, your appearance, name, gender, race, relations, situations may change, that purely depends on balancing of Karma between the two souls and time, which runs this soul travel; like we have a **Creator, Ruler, Destroyer** to run this world, the same concept **Karma, Dharma and Time** play in this soul travel. In this conversation, we didn't realize that we were discussing about it for the past three hours.

We don't know time is passing when our comfort zone is not disturbed.

After checking the time, Malini said, "I need to go as I have some daily activities." I tried to ask her, 'Why are you into prostitution and these activities when you know this much stuff related to life and world?' But, I didn't question her because I couldn't gather enough courage with fear of it resulting in some disturbances in our relation. I started respecting her, giving a good weightage to her words. She was paying the bill for the food we ate, I didn't stop her and felt comfortable, maybe this comfort with her arose because of that respect which I got for her then.

She stood from her chair with a smile, indicating that she needed to leave from there. Then, I asked her when could we meet again, as we didn't have any contact between us then. She started saying, "Don't worry, Madan. All this conversation in our relationship till now was without any contact, we have one location where I daily come to and complete my daily task. You can meet me there when you need me," and left the café.

Maybe her being mentally reserved kept back our further meeting plans aside. I was looking at her from back; she was walking out of the café. Those visuals before me were being recorded so strongly in my mind, maybe because of that fresh slice of respect I developed for her. When respect for someone rises in our IN ME, we feel so humble towards that person and see all their greatness. And with that humility and greatness, I decided not to meet her anymore.

I thought that this was something to be remembered for a long time, I needed to carry this feeling of impression of hers for a long time in my life, this respect for her must be felt and celebrated in my IN ME for a long time. Further meetings with her might bring down or raise that respect for her, so I didn't want to disturb that respect for her. This respectful feeling for her could help me build up confidence in her Soul Travel concept in my IN ME, which could make me believe and look upon Mrudhula' s soul travel with my soul.

This Soul travel's impact on me made decide not to meet her there anymore, and then I was realizing that respect for her was also because of the precious thought of further connecting souls and it made me satisfied by imagining and looking at the situation from Out of the Box; that we are separated physically and connected with Souls.

I went back to Sharma uncle and conveyed to him that I needed to go back home, "Please do the arrangements, I have some work there." He was a bit confused from my version and conveyed the same to my father, but after speaking on telephone with me, my father got that flavour of confidence from my words and asked Sharma uncle to arrange tickets for Delhi to Visakhapatnam.

Mrs. Sharma, after listening to all this conversation from inside, came out by saying, "Madan, this is very nice to listen to and I can sense that confidence in your words after all these days here on your trip. I guess something good has happened and you usefully explored here in Delhi, which would be helpful to you in kick-starting your life." I smiled and said yes to her, also realizing the power of women again from her."

Mr. Sharma & my father were two Men involved in carrying the dutiful work by doing those needful activities, but Mrs. Sharma was one woman again, who got that pinch of development happening to me, in my IN ME.

I think the women in a Man's life come in by many relations, in many ways, they play a major role in developing and transforming us. We men think women are dependent on us, but the fact we comfortably ignore is that a Woman is that power we men always depend on and right from the birth, Every man is a creation of multitude of Women in different phases of life.

I concluded my Delhi Trip with this experience in my life and stepped out to Visakhapatnam.

December 2012 – 7 years later in my Life

It's now Seven years from that departure from Delhi to Visakhapatnam.

With

Many changes,

Many learnings,

Many conclusions,

Many commitments,

Many friends,

Many failures,

Many achievements,

Many learnings,

Many memories,

Many intentions,

I completed 26 years of my life with these many alterations, ups and downs, life thoughts and all these made me experience and realize:

We must have plans to do something in life

If we succeed, our success will take us further,

If we fail it will decide how to do things further,

Success and failure complete the heartbeat of life; we must have both to continue life.

Today we may have difficulties; tomorrow we may have many more difficulties, but if we stand despite that, then the day after tomorrow will be beautiful.

Many happenings in my life took me to another level of maturity.

I come out from my thoughts of this past period of my life

and realize that my wife is in the critical care unit of the hospital.

Doctor Ayesha is treating her by monitoring her condition continuously. Physically, I was comfortable sitting on this chair for hours and recollecting, but mentally I am meshed with many thoughts.

I go down and quickly have a review of the current happenings and find the same critical care monitoring without much progress in her health. My father is the strongest pillar standing with me at this moment and is taking care of everything and made me feel better, comfortable and harmonious.

By keeping my thoughts on hold, by keeping that starting phase of 2012 from my past where I had met my wife in my life, I go back to that chair which has been giving much comfort to me for the past few hours.

2012, this was the year she came into my life and became my strength and she had become my

Half Vision
Complete Life & Double Strength

Those were the days in Varanasi, when I had joined as a senior executive of Sales in a branch office of M/s Castle foods located near Kashi Vishwanath temple area with a positive aura all over with good working staff and reporting staff. As I had newly joined the organization, they were planning to send me to our corporate quarters for a couple of weeks for the purpose of orientation training of our organization. Also, I was advised to make clearance of all the welfare related facilities and accommodation issues; to be settled and cleared in the corporate office only.

Wander Walks

Mrs. Akshara was the head of administration in the corporate office, looking upon all the admin related operations in all locations. I was told that she was

strict, a feminist, impatient, very competent, rude, harsh and a rebel kind of lady. We were told to be careful in our every conversation with her. She had a good touch in assessing employees by their body language, more than their vocal language. This was the feedback I was fed by my colleagues and other staff who had an experience with her. I was almost out and scared after hearing about her and was a bit scared to face her because I had listened to some examples from my colleagues about her ego and hatred for male dominance. Also, I got to know she was much egoistic and hurting her ego may lead to keeping our welfare request file pending for months to a year. I was thinking of how to tackle her, as per these unanimous one-sided feedbacks which I got from my colleagues. I couldn't get or find any way to tackle her.

Keeping all this aside, I had a good time to spend after office hours, in which I started exploring Varanasi and the outskirts of Varanasi. In India, this is one of the holy and blessed lands; culture in Varanasi was very pleasant, heart touching and created feelings of closeness towards the heart, the fragrance of the soil on this land maintained much of a positive aura with the essence of past and progressive nature in the present.

The oldest city in the world with a combination where,

Yesterday's beliefs can't be challenged and Tomorrow`s science can be witnessed in Varanasi.

You may be the master of your life but you can't make a choice to Perish or be born in Varanasi.

Everyday illuminates with the manifestation of truth and reveals the reality of life.

Every moment of life here celebrates with the Supreme and travels within that narrow path to Moksha.

Great Ganga flowing here is the symbol of kindness in

Humanity and gives a gist of fearlessness in honesty.

Equality as a way and innocence as nature.

Epitome of Knowledge and Moral of non-materialistic happiness.

Varanasi is the Start of every end & end of every start.

I reached office, usually had interactions, meetings, reviews with my team, had lunch, had fun in life in after office hours, and my daily routine continued like this for weekdays. One day, I got the notice to attend orientation training in the corporate office and make things clear with Mrs. Akshara. I started towards the corporate office in Kolkata and reached to our company accommodated guest house. I was going to our corporate office in Rajarhat area. After a long and good gap, I was seeing Kolkata again. Much developed and clean' was the impression I made during the visit this time.

I checked in to the corporate office, met the concerned officials and started the induction training activities. On a serious note, I didn't know much about this company nor did

I enquire before joining because of the turnover and brand value of the company in the market, my IN ME convinced to join and take the responsibilities. But in the orientation, there were some great accomplishments of organization shared with us to get a good working impression of the company, and meeting some of our reporting officials daily and enjoying the daily night life was included in the routine of my daily training period in Kolkata.

A lady was shouting on some subordinates for work and her voice was coming out from a closed cabin. I was surprised to listen to that shouting and that too in a corporate office. I tried to see who was that and which cabin was that. Akshara Shrivastava was written on its door, this made me recollect all the examples of many incidents which my colleagues had shared with me in the past. I didn't try to spend much time near this cabin and walked away by thinking how to face her and how to get the things done; handling her to get things done was my next biggest task.

Walking away from her cabin and thinking how to interact with her, I forgot half of my requirements after seeing this situation. I reached the balcony of the office and one lady standing there saw me for a while and walked inside the office. I didn't care much amid this mixed feeling and tension of getting the things done. Till now, my training phases were going well without much disturbance with a good nightlife. I sat on a chair on the balcony, thinking of all these mixed thoughts, and I finally decided to check who were her close associates in order get the things done by maintaining some good rapport with them. I had kept my mobile in charging on the desk and started thinking all these things while sitting in the balcony. Suddenly, I heard the ringtone of my mobile kept on my desk. Hurriedly, I was walking towards my mobile from balcony to the desk in the office, and I was abruptly greeted by, "Hi, are you Madan?" These were the words in a lady's voice. I listened to it from my side, I looked back to check who she was. She was that lady who saw me for a while just a few minutes ago, in the balcony.

She: Are you Madan?

Me: Yes, but who are you?

She: Your father is Mr. Murthy, right?

I was mute and started looking at her confusedly.

She: You have one sister and your mother is a Finance analyst, right?

Me: How do you know all these things?

She: You are from Visakhapatnam, right?

Me: Yes, who are you, how do you know all this? Have you checked my details in my joining form?

She: Don't you remember me?

(My IN ME was not getting any clue on who was this beautiful looking girl who was speaking out all my basic details confidently.)

She: Don't think much. Just tell me, do you remember me?

Me: Are you serious or pranking me with my details which you got from the joining form?

She: Okay, you liked to spend your time in the water and once in your childhood, you were drowned in the swimming pool, right?

Me: Yes, how do you know, who said this to you?

She: Did you mention these things in your joining form?

Me: No, but I cannot recollect who you are and I am unable to connect to any memory with you.

She: Yes, you cannot remember me, but I can never forget you in my life.

Me: What a strange version is this? What happened and what did I do?

She: Don't you remember me; don't you remember what you did?

Me: Sorry, please stop pranking with me, who are you?

She: Do you remember a girl in your childhood with whom you misbehaved, at an age of approximately 5 or 6 years?

Me: What? How do you know this deepest and never recollected memory from the depth of my heart?

She: Yes, I too couldn't remember or recollect this if I had listened to this from someone else, but I am the one who experienced this with you.

Me: Seriously? Don't tell me you are Mythili!

She: Yes, now tell me, do I know you and do you know me, what you have been asking for a few minutes now.

Me: I can't believe this; you remember this incident with me.

She: How can any girl forget this? That too at the age of five years and we were neighbours till we completed our class three in St. Joseph school.

Me: Sorry, that was so embarrassing to me then and is even now.

She: What are you doing here and why are you here?

Me: I recently joined this organization as a senior executive in sales in the regional office at Varanasi and I came here for an orientation training. What about you? Are you working here now?

She: Yes, I am working as a special officer here in the corporate office and I am touring to all regional offices to monitor the basic operations.

Me: Very nice, great meeting you. This is something embarrassing and nostalgic to me. I don't know how to handle this moment now, but I'm loving this!

She: Don't worry, you handled well. Also remember, I will not and I cannot forget what you are embarrassed for.

My mobile started ringing one more time on my desk. This phone call broke our conversation and I went to pick up the call. After the phone call, I was searching for where she was with a little excitement to explore some more discussion between us, but she was in the conference hall with some employees. Maybe, she was attending a meeting. I remained quiet and walked away by thinking I must have taken her mobile number that time.

I started walking towards Mrs. Akshara's cabin to check who were her close associates in the office to make some good friends and get my pending work done. There, I saw Mythili inside the cabin, discussing something with Akshara. After seeing this, I stepped back because I wouldn't have felt good if Akshara started shouting or rejecting my proposal in front of Mythili.

Engaged in working on a monthly sales report on my desk, I was completely involved in calculating, analysing the report, and there was a female voice from my back who asked me to take some water to drink. I turned back to check who was offering me water and disturbing me from my calculation and analysis part; It was Mythili with a smiling face and said, "both of us couldn't continue our previous conversation because of your phone call," She said, "you are a good artist." She started talking about my drawings which I presented at various events in the last 3 years (after Mrudhula's incident, I had started developing drawing as my hobby).

I asked,

Me: How do you know this? Who told you, I didn't even mention this in my joining form?

She: There's no need to check your joining form to know about you Madan, no form of you can consist of these many details which I know about you.

Me: Hey Mythili, stop saying this. I am confused and already embarrassed about the things which happened between you and me in our childhood. Though they were not big, but remembering them now are making me embarrassed.

She: Cool, don't worry, don't get panicked too.

Me: Nothing like that. Generally, I used to analyse people and take some inputs of them from their body language and intent of the words they spoke, but now you are saying many things about me without my knowledge, this made me think much.

She: Don't worry, I won't keep you in suspense for more seconds. I will tell you how I know this and what more I know about you.

A couple of years back, I came to Visakhapatnam to my granny's house and saw you there in one painting exhibition. You were involved in arranging your paintings in order at the stall allocated to you. I tried to recollect who you were, your face was somewhat familiar in my thoughts, but was not able to get who you were. I tried a lot to recollect from my thoughts. After a while, memories of first standard section "A" flashed in front of my eyes and I recollected many more memories that made me recollect all those childhood days, our games, our houses, locations where our families went for shopping, how we used to quarrel for that robot toy, how you misbehaved with me once on our terrace and I complained about you to your parents and went to my home crying. I still remember that punishment which your father gave you in front of me. Then, I started to think about your whereabouts, and contacted our old school friends to get your details, but none of my friends were in contact with you nor they knew about your whereabouts also. I couldn't get any mutual friends from our colony neighbours also. Thus, I didn't get any clue from our notebooks, friends or even neighbours. And then, after three days of my searches and enquiries about you, I came to the exhibition again with a thought to meet you directly, but the exhibition got closed, and I again missed your contact. Started to search you on Orkut by your name and your likes of interests which I knew and remembered about you. I searched in many Orkut communities related to painting and arts, but I couldn't get you there, I tried to search you on ORKUT PSPK community too.

"Stop it, what is this PSPK community on Orkut?"

"Don't you know this? Power star Pawan Kalyan community in Orkut which is one of the most active and top communities in India, where thousands of active members visit daily and interact, origin of Pawanism is this ORKUT PSPK" She said.

"Oh, I have heard about this. Though I am also a follower of Pawan Kalyan, but didn't know much about ORKUT PSPK," I said and asked her more, in order to continue with my inner excitement which arose by listening to my childhood crush expressing about me.

She continued saying about exploring on Facebook and on other social media networks too, "As I didn't know your surname, it took much time to explore you. Finally, I got your profile after trying to search all our school friends from the school page. I came to know what are you doing, where you are and who are my known friends in contact with you."

"This is something nice that someone tried to know about me," I said to her. Immediately, with a sharp nose, she started looking at me seriously by saying, "Am I that someone to you?" I laughed and answered her "Not really, Miss Mythili madam,"

There was a call from Akshara madam, to Mythili and Akshara madam saw me discussing with Mythili. I guess this was the first time she was seeing me, I was a bit afraid from her look and the impression I had on her, and the requirement I had with her.

Mythili came out after meeting and discussing with her, we started our discussion, then she asked about my whereabouts in Kolkata and in Varanasi. Then, I started talking about my frustration to fall out with my worry and pain to her, regarding accommodation and other welfare facilities I needed to get from Akshara madam. Also, regarding the stories I heard about her and the impression I had on her. I thought she understood my concern and worry as I was a newcomer in this organization.

She smiled broadly after listening to my version on Akshara and said,

"Not that bad, Madan, you have listened to an almost correct version on her. Don't worry, give me some time, I will make the things done for you" and she walked away to Akshara's cabin. Though I didn't expect any help from her, but she assured me to get the things done and returned with a house allotment letter in Varanasi for entitlement of all the welfare parts which I needed to get in our organization. I was in such a condition which was near to surprise, and was happy also a bit, nearer to the excitement of getting the things done very easily.

We don't know the value of situations when we get the things done, but we come to know the value of people who stood with us unconditionally to get the things done. This unexpected support from her made me think about and listen to her.

There was a call from Akshara madam, to Mythili. This time she was going again to her cabin, but the way I started seeing her changed, she was walking away from me now. I was seeing her back constantly; she was now looking like a stiff lady soldier in that grey pants and white shirt attire. Mythili was about 5 feet 8-inch tall with slim to moderate personality, medium length of hair and whose smiling lips brought a charm on her face. Her confidence was always reflected in her body language which made her eyes more intense than that of the other ladies I had seen in the recent years. Her oratory skills made her more expressive; oratory skills were an added advantage to her confidence, definitely making her a woman of power and charm.

I was back to my work of compiling the sales reports and mesh full of papers on my desk. Calculating, and analysing the reports involved me so much into the work, that I kept working without thinking of the scenario that happened between Mythili and me. After a while, I was stuck with the mismatch in reports which made me to rework, with utter load I was correcting reports. The office boy kept a cup of coffee on my desk and went away. As I didn't have a habit of drinking coffee or tea, I must have said to him that I didn't need this coffee, but due to this work and mismatch of calculations in report I didn't react quickly. I was calling him to say that this coffee was not required as I didn't drink coffee, but my voice was not high enough and he didn't listen to it. One of my colleagues saw this and came near me with a smile and took the cup of coffee by saying, "I will take it if you don't mind." I said, "That's nice," and handed my cup of coffee to him, kept my work on hold for a while as he started to chit chat with me and gradually his conversation led to some indirect questions about the conversation between me and Mythili. He later asked me, "How do you know Mythili madam, she generally don't speak much with anyone because she is the only daughter of our Managing director of this Castle Foods."

"What?" I paused him with shock, "What are you saying?"

He started narrating the role of Mythili in the office, "As she is the only daughter of our Managing Director, she is about to take over this organization soon. Meanwhile, to know about the basic middle-level management, she is involved in the corporate office activities, she is very smart and an efficient lady and takes care of every employee in professional and personal terms, there are many examples where she took the personal responsibilities of some of our staff members working here for the last 10 years. All the elder or long term associated employees of this group consider her as their daughter, more than their boss."

This conversation with my colleague made me blank and everything seemed unbelievable. I thought I must take time to gather enough courage to talk to Mythili, more than Akshara.

Mythili was my childhood friend and neighbour, she had said some good stuff about me and she also told the way she tried to enquire about my details from our friends. Also, I knew and had seen her father from my childhood days, 'how come I didn't know this, even my parents also never discussed about them, as they were our neighbours once upon a time.'

With many confusing conclusions, I completed the office hours that day and reached the guest house and continued thinking a lot and cooked stuff about this in my IN ME.

Next day, in the office, I was engaged in my work. Mythili was sitting in the conference hall, attending meeting on some issues. Previously also, I had seen her attending meetings in that conference hall, but now my way of looking at her was different and slightly afar from my thoughts. I carried on with my work till lunch and thought to walk for lunch at a nearby restaurant that day. Mythili saw me walking out of the office towards the restaurant and called me to come back. I said, "I am walking to have lunch in the restaurant." In reply, she said, she would be joining me for lunch in the restaurant then. I was paused due to my unclear thoughts in my IN ME and stood silent.

We sat and ordered food. It would have taken 20 minutes to get the food served. I was mute and she was slightly ok with her work and conveyed some meeting discussion points to me. I couldn't understand how to react as I had many thoughts of keeping her away after knowing that she was the daughter of our managing director.

I think she understood the change in my level of comfort and therefore, asked me, "What happened, why are you a bit tensed and mute, what are you thinking, what made you so silent?"

Me: I heard that your father is the managing director of this company.

She: Yes, So?

Me: Nothing, this is keeping me a bit distant from you. I am taking time to respond to every word of yours.

She: Come on, Madan. Don't take it as this, you are not an outsider nor I am a stranger to you. Also, I am not looking at you as our employee, you're my best person and you are that only person in my life I tried to remember, whom I tried to know about. Though we didn't have any contact or any conversation between us, but maybe because of our childhood and the things happened then in those days made me look for you, know about you, but I never tried to meet you in person.

I was drinking water and listening to her without any reply.

She continued saying, "The day I saw you in the office was like a miracle of life. I never had a thought or intention to meet you but the destiny of my life made a map towards you, this is what I felt when I saw you."

Me: I know you are clever and have studied in one of the top IIMs in this country, you have a brilliant IQ, but what made you have so silly thoughts like this for me. I can understand that emotion from our childhood had an impact on you and also on me but I can't believe that emotion is the sole reason of this feeling for a girl like you.

She: Keep patience, Madan. I said I know much about you; I have done good enquiry about you even before we met. When I started knowing about you, I started with that emotion from our childhood only, but later I came to know many things, many versions of you, many life lessons from you which you witnessed. Now, I am clear about you and I know many of those things about you and also between you and Mrudhula and that phase you went through, the lesson which life taught you.

Me: How do you know about Mrudhula?

She: I said I know much about you. Keep patience, Madan. When I started enquiring about you, the stories of your school days and high school days were very interesting and made me feel nice towards you. I felt your character was like a *sky kept under the terrace,* but when I continued exploring you from engineering days, then I came to know all about you and about the rebels and the bad seeds. Your activities on child labour to rescuing girls from nearby villages. Also, about your heart and lady love, Miss Mrudhula and relations between you both before the incident happened.

Me: Who told you all this? Only limited people know about Mrudhula.

She: Excuse me, Madan sir, keep patience and let me complete. Next, I tried to know the people in your life after Mrudhula's incident in 2005 and again I got the contact of a few people who are in your life since 2008. I continued exploring you again and I came to know about your hard phases of diversion from depression. Here came your political activities, your support to politicians during the election in Visakhapatnam, your charities, your interest in painting and getting that pain out of you through your paintings and completing your MBA and then starting your professional career in other FMCG company, to the present of you sitting with me in this restaurant for lunch.

Me: This, I can't believe. I seriously felt happy yesterday when you conveyed that you tried to know about me, but now that happiness has turned into fear on listening to this, relating to all timelines of my life. ***How can a man take his version from a woman that too surprisingly without his intervention?***

She: Don't worry. The food is here and let's have food. We finished lunch and returned back to the office. People in the office started looking at us with a special vision and particularly, special vision for me because she was the boss in the office and I was their colleague. Obviously, anyone would misunderstand and think of reasons for Mythili spending time with me among all groups and departments in the office. And this relation with Mythili after office hours and dinners in the restaurants started and continued for three days. I witnessed her passion, brilliance and excellence of her thought process. This impressed me and made me a bit comfortable with her. We continued shopping clothes and gifts for each other, her taste of selection of gifts was very creative.

The Day had come to leave Kolkata and head to Varanasi as my orientation training had got completed and now I had to join back at our regional office. I came blank to Kolkata and was returning with mixed emotions to Varanasi. I packed my luggage and was about to start from the guest house to the Dumdum international airport, when I got a call from Mythili expressing best wishes and happy journey and she then shut the call. My IN ME started missing her and I started thinking about her. Though this relationship was directed towards getting her into my life, after seven years, my heart and brain got some sense in my thoughts and feelings, it was like a water drop in Oasis after seven years.

I reached the airport and settled my luggage in the trolley. I realised there was someone holding my bag and trying to keep it on my trolley. I just checked who that was, it was Mythili who had come to the airport to give a send-off. But surprisingly, I saw some extra baggage with her. She kept that on my trolley which was completely filled and the bags were about to fall from the trolley if I moved. I asked her, "What is this luggage and why are you keeping it on my trolley and whose luggage is this?" She kept an A4 size folded paper in my hands and asked me to read, that was her ticket to Varanasi from Kolkata in the same flight. I was surprised and happy to see this, but some unanswered questions arose and thus I asked, "why are you coming and when did you plan this, are you ok with this travel now?"

"Yes, I am ok," she said and conveyed that her trip was related to, a visit to our regional office in Varanasi. I was surprised to listen to that and asked her, "Why didn't you tell this to me before?"

She said, "I wanted to see the happiness on your face directly when you'd come to know that I am joining you."

Me: How did you think that happiness would be my reaction?
She: I understand you Madan and especially after knowing you, your last few years of life are so nice and honest in my view.

Me: Along with happiness, I also have tension in my mind. Some of our colleagues came to know about our frequent conversations in the office. This might result in people commenting on you, as you are the daughter of the Managing director. There may be many spices added up to the real version of what we really are, Mythili.

She: Don't worry about this Madan. I have already conveyed to my father about my trip and interaction with you. He felt very happy on hearing about you and your family. Also, he recollected some good memories from his past in Visakhapatnam. He also recollected those childhood mischief activities. He remembered that in one event during dinner, unknowingly, your plate slipped and dal fell on his shirt and in the middle of the party he had to go back home to change the shirt and then return. Also, some incidents related to our exams every month and progress card marks with comparison among both our families and many such memories are there in his head.

Me: Nice, so uncle remembers all these. Oh sorry, now he is my boss, I must call him sir, so sir remembers all this and that's great!

She: Let us proceed for the boarding pass section.

She tried to move the trolley which was filled completely with luggage.

Me: Let's take one more trolley, else baggage may fall from the trolley.

She: Don't worry, I will handle this.

She continued dragging the trolley till the boarding pass section.

We stood in a line to get the boarding pass and she stood before me in the line. I started thinking about her from the moment she took that trolley from me to handling it till the boarding pass section. It was like successfully handling our mixed responsibilities of this one life with utmost care. I felt that baggage were our responsibilities in life and that trolley resembled my life; overfilled with the responsibilities I couldn't handle. She made it easy for me, as of now, I was not clear on thinking of my life with her, but now thoughts in my IN ME started.

We reached Varanasi and I joined back the office with a proud feeling in front of my colleagues that I got the work done from Akshara madam in one attempt, and all those were surprised and did not believe my words. I showed that letter which Mythili had given me on that day, some felt happy and some felt jealous on witnessing the work done in the first attempt with Akshara madam in our corporate office. A couple of days slowly flew from the calendar where the strategies and tasks handed to me were clear and the work initiated. The work in the office was getting smoother and was improving day by day, and my habit of meeting Mythili daily before office hours at the bank of river Ganga had developed as my daily practice. We used to travel by boat from temple side to the opposite side of the river to witness the sunrise from the opposite side to temple and discuss many happenings in our lives.

Every alternate day, we attended Ganga Arti and spent our time in devotion of Mahadev BoleNath and Lord Shiva Parvathi and we used to discuss many aspects of human life and our lives.

Unknowingly, I was involved in discussion and thoughts of our lives, our thoughts started by clubbing both the lives, our plans started by involving both lives, unknowingly she was a happening part of my life. Keeping the possibility aside, we were both involved in planning our lives.

One morning, after I reached the banks of river Ganga, I got a call from her, "Today, I have a meeting and I need to attend it, so it's not possible to meet today and let's meet tomorrow a bit earlier." I, alone spent time and enjoyed the fresh breeze and thought to paint and create a portrait of the visuals before me. Though many great artists from centuries were painting this great place, the Ghats, the temples, the river, and the activities here, but I was thinking to bring out something which was not brought by any one till now. Involved in thinking to bring that creative part out of me and create the beautiful portrait, I walked inside a small village located at the side of the river. The early morning walks in Varanasi were really a blessing of supreme devotion all around; tea in mud cups, divinity in all the faces I was seeing, many pandits, sadhus and fragrance of dhoop-dhuni in the air, small idols and shivlings in temples in the village and to witness devotion in the eyes of those people offering *pooja* early mornings during sunrise. Witnessing all this purity on earth was truly a gift and blessing of the Almighty, the supreme Lord Shiva.

Meanwhile, I found two groups of people arguing for some reason, it made my legs to stick there. I stood there and witnessed their arguments and tried to decode their issue. Gradually, the people were increasing and turning like a mob with arguments. I was much involved in listening to them like all other visitors to that place. The argument was something related to local and non-local issue on employment in some industry. I was seriously involved in listening to their versions by folding my hands and patiently looking into their eyes who were arguing and I was trying to know their intense argument. I started judging their points in my IN ME. Forty minutes had passed, I was still listening and they were still arguing. No one in this surrounding tried to mediate between these groups. As I didn't know the past history of this argument, I didn't try to involve in between to mediate. But if they were left like that, without any mediating, then that might have turned into a mob and situations could have been uncontrolled. Thoughts of my IN ME were involved in judging them from their points rolling out there.

There was some group of people who came there with bow and arrows with them. I was like, 'What the crap is happening here, why are these bow and arrows here and who are these.' As I was contemplating, the situation was turning violent with Mob as there was no one to mediate till then and thus it was too out of control to handle that.

The group of people with the bow and arrows started

releasing arrows on the people who were witnessing this. The group turned into a mob and started damaging nearby shops, hurting people by throwing empty cold drink bottles and releasing arrows. Everyone was running from the location and the crowd was disturbed, small children were crying out loud. I was still standing there with my ego of anger on that group of people releasing arrows and hurting people by throwing empty cold drink bottles. I knew, in my past, I had controlled multiple disturbed events like this, but there I couldn't control because there was no enough morality left in me as I didn't know the history of this disturbed mob and I couldn't judge who was correct and who was wrong. So that honesty in my IN ME was not getting boosted which was important for me to take decisions. Within a few minutes, the entire area was cleared with fear and damaged with agony of few selfish, sick people there.

After a while, I was the only person standing there. All others who remained from that mob wore dhoti, and I was the only man dressed oddly wearing jeans and shirt. They all focussed on me and started shouting at me. The angry mob might have attacked me because the issue was with local and non-local on employment in the industry. All others standing there wore dhoti, obviously I became their target and they shouted louder. Nearly 50 plus members focussed on me and a few were violently scolding me in some local language which I wasn't able to understand.

More than ten people raised their bows and targeted their arrows pointing towards me. I wasn't able to understand their language, but I could understand their intention and the next action. I started running from that location with many thoughts in my mind as I couldn't handle that situation then. If I had involved a bit earlier, then I might have handled that, but then it was very much delayed and the situation was out of my hands and I was running away from them. It was such a messy situation where I felt for the first time that I couldn't handle and started running from them.

While running, I turned back to have a look at the scenario and I saw there were more than twenty people standing in two rows and pointed their arrows towards me, who could release their arrows in any second. Running away with many thoughts in my mind, I thought these were the last seconds of my life, my chapter is closed today with these people and few memories started flashing in my mind. Still, my ego was saluting up in my thoughts saying, "Don't run and face this, go opposite to them." But my IN ME was saying "this is not the thing in which you are involved. Just run from here and save yourself, there is no one in this entire location who can save you."

The mob which aimed the arrows on me had lost their senses due to anger and dominance. Few seconds passed and I was running, then I got the doubt that why didn't they release the arrows on me still? What made them to take this much time to hurt me? I turned back to witness what was happening behind my back. There I saw a miracle, an older man, aged more than seventy years with white hair, white beard came scolding the mob in their language and tried to stop the release of arrows pointed towards me. Those who pointed the arrows from the mob were listening to him. I didn't know what was happening and what they were discussing, but without waiting, I escaped from there to a nearby place where I saw some people. I ran out from there up to 3 kilometers to get to some good place where people were normal and involved in their daily activities. I stopped there for a while and took some rest to get down my breathlessness, to make myself stable and to get down that sweat on me. I finally found a shop having shelter and a bench to sit. I called Mythili and conveyed everything which happened in last one hour and explained how I ran from there and where I was then. She immediately sent the security team of our organization to the location where I was sitting and they took me back to the office in their vehicle safely without any further disturbance. I must thank that older man who came in between to stop that angry mob and gave some space for me to escape. I didn't know who he was and did not see his face to remember. In just a fraction of seconds all that had happened and then I was about to reach our office with our organization's security team.

Mental Romance

In a while, Mythili came to me and asked about the incident in detail and stood beside me for an hour to make me comfortable and normal. After an hour, I involved myself in my work and continued working till evening. Mythili told me that we would have dinner in a restaurant outside and shared the location and time, and asked me to join there.

I reached the location; it was a shopping mall with a celebratory environment all over and had many stalls with different types of ambience all across. There I saw Mythili on the second floor and we walked into a restaurant. It was like a theme-based retro restaurant; live musical concert on the side stage and main stage was left as a dance floor. Customers were enjoying like they had no worries. The dance floor was filled with customers in the restaurant and they were dancing to that live music which was arranged on the side stage. I loved this theme based retro restaurant, and I started walking behind Mythili and she was walking to a table. We settled on such a table from where we both could view the activities on the dance floor on the main stage and live music activities on side stage. The music was rocking to its best in the restaurant. We ordered food and were enjoying the sequence of classical songs with live music and dance on the main stage floor.

"This restaurant is really nice to spend some time," said Mythili to me. . I kept quiet and looked into her eyes, her eyes had that charm of achievement. She also started looking into my eyes, her eyes were as if smiling by looking into my eyes, but my eyes were intense somehow. We both kept quiet and continued looking for a few seconds, this was like our souls were kissing with eyes. The charm in her smiling eyes increased, my intense-looking eyes had lost before her smiling eyes, and breaking this kiss, I spoke,

Me: What happened?

She: What happened?

Me: Why are you kissing me with your eyes?

She: I don't know. You started this first and I continued along with the comfort.

Me: No, I was not kissing in the starting, but that charm in your smiling eyes made me lose the intensity in my eyes and I started kissing you.

She: I don't think so. There was no intensity in your eyes, rather I saw some sort of insecurity in your eyes.

Me: (after a pause for few seconds) Yes, you are right.

She: Why Madan, what made you have such insecurities with me?

Me: Maybe, I am wrong Mythili, but,

I am not comfortable with you because mentally, you are much superior to me,

You know every major aspect of my life,

Your concern for me is higher than my concern for you,

Your love for me is like a mountain and my love is like a stone before your mountain-sized love,

You think a lot about my wellbeing,

You are much superior to me in terms of academics & maturity,

You have much better IQ than me,

Your thoughts are much broader than mine,

I am such kind of a guy that I can never let myself down before anyone, I can never approach anyone for any sort of help, but before you, all my skills are not enough to save my skin.

Rather than expecting, I always give the best to everyone, but your normal is even delivering better than my best.

My attitude is like a wall of support to everyone, but your wall of support to me is bigger than mine.

I am superior to the entire world surrounding me, but to me, you are much superior,

I took the concern of many, but never felt the concern for anyone. But now, your love and concern are huger than mine.

I am the best and the greatest in my world, but you are double great than me.

I am saying this to you again, I may be wrong, but I could neither take this nor let you go away from my life. My wanting of you in my life is more than you want me in your life. My intention is not to hurt you, I am trying to get some solution for my insecurities with you because I couldn't get the solution for these. Thus, now I am again dependent on you to bring me out from these insecurities.

She listened to this completely without any word in reply; she took a deep breath and smiled with a light lip movement. The waiter brought the ordered food and kept it on the table. We silently had the food without any discussion. The rocking music and dancing crowd around us were not making any impact on us after my conversation. We just had our dinner while all the people around us were celebrating this moment.

I think I spoiled that evening by opening up myself regarding all this. "Mythili, I am sorry," I conveyed to her while having dinner. She just smiled and replied, "Nothing like that Madan," and continued having her dinner without any word again. I was seeing her eyes now filled with many emotions and slightly watery. I felt bad for opening up on these feelings of mine before her, but at the other corner of my IN ME, it was like, 'Nothing is wrong, you are genuine Madan. You didn't lie to her, nor cheated her, so cheer up and be confident of your honesty in this relation.'

My IN ME started rewinding all those moments and learnings of my life beginning from the school days. I was realizing that most of my learning was with various women with various relations in this life. Starting from my school days, many women teachers taught me the best things apart from education, they taught me well on behaving and communicating. ***Though men are physically strong, women are mentally stronger and clearer than men***, *this may be the reason why most of the schools keep lady teachers than male ones in kindergarten to medium-high school classes*, then came the role of various 'Sirs' who made us disciplined in our lives. Mentally strengthened Women are the base of every initiation and physically strengthened men are protectors of that solid base made by those women in our lives.

Fifteen minutes had elapsed, we were silently having dinner while sitting opposite to each other. The entire confession, I made to her was running in my mind. She was silently having her dinner with emotional drizzled eyes. The music was rocking around us and this celebration mode in the restaurant and those dancing moves to live music was not making any impact on this situation between us. We were just involved in our world of thoughts. I was thinking to have a word with her and start a conversation to divert the intentions and situations that developed in the last thirty minutes.

There was a group of event managers with video recording cameras and mikes along with an anchor approaching the people in the restaurant randomly and asking kinky random questions related to lifestyle and relationships. This activity made me turn my head towards those questions. After a few minutes, they came to our table and greeted us with a warm smile and kept the mike before me, whereas the cameras focused on me, followed by lighting,

Anchor: What's your name?

Me: Madan.

Anchor: Ok, Mr. Madan. We are conducting promotions of our restaurant on a topic of importance in relationships. Can you and madam take part in this question and answer session with us?

We looked at each other, as we are not talking to each other for a while. Mythili kept quiet and smiled while saying, "Okay."

Anchor: What do you think, in a relationship, who plays the major role?

Me: Both the man and the woman play an equal role.

(The anchor kept the mike in front of Mythili for the same question)

Mythili: As Madan said, both play an equal role.

Anchor: Great. Who actually balances the relation when you have a phase of disturbances or downs?

Me: (This was something near to our situation now) It's a hypothetical question, it depends on the experience. Now the answer varies with case to case, but in most of the relations I have seen, I believe that the Men are Physically stronger and Women are mentally strong. We, men, are like stones in the relationship, whereas women are that sculptors who shape out the stone and work hard to get that beautiful output. We, men, may get frustrated or are fed up after some days in our relationships by losing patience and we feel that all the hardships in the life are because of the woman only. However, we don't realize the woman is that strength and driving force in a relationship which brings out the beautiful output (happy life). Though a woman gives us hardship, a woman gives us the feeling of dominance, a woman may give a sense of superiority over man in a relation, but even she faces the same hardship as us and even takes the same pain as we do. We, men, are mentally weak and expel out easily for some sort of concern from a woman because we feel it as restrictions. Still, a woman is that mentally strong driving force which will hold us, bear with us and take us to the beautiful phase of life.

Anchor: "This is something very great I listened to today," She thanked me for this message and kept the mike towards

Mythili and asked, "Mr. Madan had said wonderful lines on balancing a relation and also gave more weightage to women, now please tell us, what according to you brings more respect and charm for you in your relation or for women in any relationship?"

Mythili: In our relation, Madan always gave my space to me and weightage too as you have witnessed in his version, but in any other relation, which I fairly and regularly observe in relations of many of my friends is, "Women must respect each other." Yes, I mean it. In many relations, women are the only enemy of women, men really don't dare to poke or degrade women until and unless other women enter and support the man. That unity among women needs to develop homogeneously and sustain with a respect towards each other, without this we can't expect women will get enough weightage in any relation. Without this respect among each other, we women are always weak and less weighted in any relation.

Anchor: Wow, again that's great listening to you Miss. Mythili. Yes, I totally agree with you. We, Women, need to have respect amongst ourselves, without any scope of getting or giving signs of weakness to men in any relation. She greeted us with the same warm smile and dispersed with the team of camera and lighting.

Now some sort of relaxation was witnessed in Mythili's eyes. She was not so particular about things, but definitely, my version about her dominance caused some discomfort to her. She started looking at me again casually and tried to smile directly by facing me.

These direct smiles towards me gave me some relaxation and I slowly started coming into our surrounding world. Stress in my IN ME came down, and the surrounding world was rocking like before; the pace of celebrations had increased than before and the dancing *josh* on the floor had reached heights. I felt relaxed, rested back on the chair and kept my left leg on right knee and started witnessing those celebrations with a feel that, 'Yes, situations are normal and under our control.'

By witnessing these celebrations, I started realizing how a woman again is the reason for my mental peace. I started wondering how my mental condition was dominated by stress and thought about her emotional eyes before few minutes. I wondered what was that relaxation I was getting with her normal eyes and what could be the level of celebration in the coming minutes if she manifested those smiling eyes again.

I was then waiting for her to come back from normal eyes to-Smiling eyes to get involved in any celebration around us there. The sequence of songs playing were very energetic, classic and equally romantic with some party mode. The sequence was like a party song followed by an old Bollywood classic song and then followed by a romantic song.

I was involved in listening to songs and watching those dance movements of all the strangers in my surrounding world. A song from '1942-a love story' started on the live orchestra with a melodious voice, '*Ek ladki ko dekha toh aisa laga*' made the crowd go crazy and everyone was shouting. This song changed my mood completely and I started enjoying the song. Really what a beautiful moment it was, my lady was in front of me in a phase of a comeback to celebration mode from the normal mode and in parallel, a classical song started with a celebrating environment. Around this, I started to get breaths in my IN ME and I started humming the lyrics and tapping my feet with the music and I started looking at Mythili randomly while humming those beautiful lyrics. It was like I made that music team to sing this song for my lady, there were some lyrics which were apt to her. Also, there were some lyrics in the song completely opposite to her, lyrics like "*Van mein Hiran Jaise*" (like a deer in the forest) were the lines getting sung from the song, I started reciting these lyrics and commenting and Mythili could hear my voice. When that lyrics of 'Van Mein Hiran Jaise' was spelled, I laughed aloud and said to myself loudly, '*Van Mein*

Hiran nahin, Sher mere aage baiti hai.' (Not like a deer in the forest, but a Lady like Tiger was sitting in front of me). I started singing some lyrics and said loudly to myself where Mythili could have heard this, saying this to bring her back to the celebrating mood.

Jaise Nachte Mor (Like a dancing peacock) I started singing and said,

"Where is that dancing peacock? There is a chasing horse before me." These comments slowly made her angry, but she wasn't able to comment back. There were a few more punch points which I utilized from the song and lyrics. The crowd around us was going crazy with the music, humming crazily to the music and everyone was involved in dancing to the music. Maybe, that was such a moment where we could say that music is the perfect healer of heart, mind and life.

After these classical songs, it was the turn of a romantic song in the sequence. Slowly, the situation was coming into my hands and I started waiting for those romantic songs to start and I kept guessing on what could be the next romantic song. The song started which made the crowd and me go crazy again, '*Zara zara behekta hai mehekta hai*' from Rehna Hain Tera Dil Mein – RHTDM. It started with husky voice of a singer which was similar to the original's, the surrounding was in such a euphoria that Mythili also started enjoying the song by humming the tune and the lyrics slowly brew in her inside. Then came out that romantic champ from my inside and I started to hum the song along with Mythili and the hums from the crowd was like a chorus to our humming. Slowly taking the situation under my control, I tried to look directly into her eyes, but she was completely involved in humming the song and took out the special lyrics from the song. My body language changed as per the tune and music of the song and my eyes felt that huskiness of the singer's voice. Though we didn't propose each other, but shared our intentions and commitments on our lives with each other like we were committed.

I never had a bit of physical romance with any lady till then, but that celebration mode environment took me to a romantic sight with Mythili. My thoughts started imagining those lyrics. Making myself wet in the thoughts of sharing my soul with her, her humming to the song was like her soul holding my soul and taking me further to complete the thirst of incompletion. Time just flew and the song was completed. Mythili opened her eyes and started looking at me, then I saw those charming and smiling eyes. I completely felt relaxed because she was normal like before.

Crowd around me was waiting for the next song to start, as per the sequence this song should have been a dance party number. The music of the song started and this time the crowd cheered crazily with raised hands and closed fists, even Mythili felt excited after listening to that music. My feet started tapping to the music and its *jhoom barabar jhoom* title song, an ultimate dance number. Mythili came near to me and pushed me back by pushing on my chest with her fingers and started walking to the dance floor. I was thrilled to see her act of pushing me back and walking on to the dance floor and I started responding to the music. This was an ultimate Bollywood party number with trendy Punjabi style lyrics, "*Oo Beech Bajari dange lag gaye, do talwari Akhiyon ke Makhana*" (In the middle of the market there are riots, of these two swords like eyes, My Beloved), this was where the song started and Mythili surprised everyone on the floor with her dance moves from hips to neck and twisting her left hand like a peacock and right leg in curve from knee, at last she settled in such a position. It was an eye feast for all those dancing-like drunkards, her moves made everyone stop their dance and I started watching Mythili. To the next lyrics of "*O Jaan Kate Ke Jigar Kate Abb Inn Do dhari Akhiyon se Makhnaa*" ('it doesn't matter if my soul cuts or chest cuts, with those sword look alike eyes, My Beloved) She made a move by bringing down her left hand with a speed by cutting into air opposite to her eyes and then to her hip, and she made her reversed palm waving between her eyes and nose. This perfection in presenting this dance made everyone a spectator of her dance, while the music and song got started to which she hit her hip with palm by stepping a foot forward and performing to the dance number which was not just like 'WoW', it was like 'YaY'. The song continued for six minutes, everyone played the role of a spectator and for the last one-minute, special bit of the song, I along with some folks started dancing beside her for *Jhoom bara bar Jhoom Jhoom.*

We came down from the dance floor feeling breathless and sat by holding each other and laughing by looking into each other's eyes. Many of the strangers around us came to us and complimented her dance. Also, some started flirting with her, but she maturely handled everyone in that situation. After a few minutes, we felt okay with our breathlessness and walked out of the restaurant, stopped for a while and turned back looking at the restaurant with a feeling of thankfulness for this good memory and we went to the parking lot to take the bike. We reached her guest house and I dropped her at the gate of the guest house, took my helmet and kept on the tank and said to her, "Seriously, today was the best day with many mixed emotions, memories and best enjoyment after many years," She kept quiet again with those emotions filled eyes and started walking towards the gate. I was watching her from my bike, my worry started again after witnessing those eyes filled with emotions. She opened the gate, but returned fast and hugged me tightly by wrapping her arms around me and grabbing my shirt. She continued holding me, and tears started rolling down her eyes.

Mythili: I love you, Madan. Sorry if I hurt you, I Love you, I don't mean to hurt you by any of my thoughts. I Love you.
I was Surprised, thrilled, confused, but maintained silence.

Mythili: I never meant to hurt you or degrade you. You said that I am dominating you, you are feeling that superiority in me,

She now released my shirt and started saying by looking into my eyes,

"We, Indian women, always try to rise and achieve heights, but never try to think of dominating our husband,

We, Indian women, might imagine or witness the husband with other women in the past, but we never take anything in a negative sense,

We Indian women can take any sort of mental and physical pressure from the husband, but we are never able to take any kind of inferiority from the husband,

We, Indian women, always keep husband at the top place till our last breath,

We Indian women are moulded mentally by traditions and culture to look at our husbands as our superheroes."

I kept calm, I didn't understand how to console and convince her. I was completely filled with her love. I said, "Mythili, as I told you women are stronger than us, this is one example when I couldn't take the control of this situation and confess what I feel and what I mean. Definitely, I feel great about this happening now, but I am failing to convey my love for you before your love. I am literally drowned in your love and trying to come out to take a breath and then talk. I think you understand this. Also, it`s not safe for you to talk more than this at this time outside your guesthouse, let's reach our beds and continue our conversation. As of now you please go inside, it's already 11:30 pm now." I made her go inside the guesthouse comfortably and returned back to my guest house.

One week had passed with our outings in the evenings, office work in day time and Riverside meetings on early morning sun rise. We now were involved completely by thinking and designing our thinking with a concept of "Belief and Freedom" to each other. And among each other, I got a little good clarity in giving Freedom to Mythili and she was clear in believing me.

Man, always misses that Belief from the woman and Woman always misses that Freedom from the man.

We now had this clarity between each other and started thinking of conveying our relationship to our parents and get their good acceptance to our further happenings in life. We were in that comfort and had crossed the line of exploring each other. Understanding each other was the biggest task in life, and since we were done with it, so conveying and convincing our parents wasn't that big task to consider in our world.

A couple of days later, we started thinking where to start from and how to convey our relationship. I had no issue in conveying the same to my family and in my point of view, Mythili must have dealt with this sensibly. Mythili started saying, "I generally don't have any issue in my house because my father has enough trust on me and definitely he will be happy after listening to this. He basically checks the zeal of growth in the boy rather than any other thing which most of our Indian parents look for. As my father is one of those successful business men in India who started his career as a worker and rose to the top chair in a company, so he basically looks for that potential." These discussions went on which boosted our confidence.

She: It is concluded that this new year we must enjoy, we almost came to year-end and today, it's December 22nd, 2012. Let us convey our relationship to our family in January, 2013.

Me: Okay, as you say.

She: One more point to say, tomorrow is Sunday, let's go for a long ride to Allahabad. The entire trip would be hardly 250 km.

Me: Okay, that's nice. We will do this (I had thought about these celebrations before the New Year).

She: With one condition, there should not be any mobile phone or wallet with you till we complete the ride. You must come only with your driving license. Apart from your driving license there shouldn't be any piece of paper in your pocket, not even your visiting card. You must only come with your driving license tomorrow. We will start by 5:00 PM in the evening and return on Monday morning, and we can join the office from the second half.

Me: Okay, but why all these conditions? I am not getting any clear picture on this, kindly let me know what is the plan and why no mobile phone, no wallet and money, no debit cards, what are we going to do and are you sure about your plan? It's better if we discuss this once before implementing, let's just give a thought and then execute and avoid basic mismatches. I know the day after tomorrow on December 24th is my birthday, but is it really required to go like this without mobile phone also?

Mythili: I have my plans, please do as I say, my dear.

<u>(December 23rd, 2012, 5:00 PM)</u>

In blue jeans, white shirt, brown jacket and black Rayban shades, I reached the guest house where Mythili resided. At around 5:15pm, she came down, with a humorous smile, asking me, why I had brought black goggles, within an hour natural light would fail to fall and thus what was the use of goggles? I too laughed and made a cover drive to support the need of goggles and said, "These goggles on my face reflect Attitude." She smiled and checked my shirt pocket and pants pockets confirming no availability of wallet and mobile phone. After confirming, she sat on the bike. We started driving towards Allahabad. We were discussing many things on our ride. While maintaining that average speed of 60 kmph and maximum speed of 100 kmph, discussing roadside sceneries and some scenic locations, we almost reached the outskirts of Allahabad and it was hardly 20 more kilometres to reach the city and I had no idea of what we were doing.

Me: I don't have any idea of what we are doing, I don't have my mobile to check on google maps, only these highway boards are guiding us by showing the remaining distance to cover and those boards showing Kilometres are guiding us to the path of Allahabad. What are we exactly doing?

She: Stay calm, dear, we are enjoying now and this is going to be one of the best memories for us.

Me: Alright, without money, I can't imagine what next and where are we heading, don't you think I should have that concern?

Meanwhile, we reached Allahabad city and then she started guiding where to go. Within a while, we reached a 3-star hotel with nice ambience and checked in one double bedroom. I was feeling a bit discomfort and uneasiness, but did not show it to Mythili. We were into the room, with no mobile phone and no money with me, but we were together. This experience was something strange which I had never imagined. Mythili started saying that it was 9:30 pm then, by 10:15pm I must get ready and we should go out. As per her plan, we completed our dinner in the restaurant by 11:30 pm and started from the restaurant on bike with a cake box from the bakery. I asked her which flavour was the cake of. "It's our favourite flavour," she said. "How do you know my favourite flavour, it might have changed now, right?"

She smiled and replied, "Madan, it's our favourite flavour from hearts, not from Lips." We started in that direction where she was guiding me to reach. After a few minutes of the journey, we reached to the Riverside, we were walking on the banks of river Ganga and Yamuna. There was a good lighting arrangement at the location where we were walking and a team of men was waiting for us. Mythili discussed something with them and in a while a boat came to us. We boarded and the boat started moving on the river. We reached at the middle of the river and she told me, "This is Sangam, Triveni Sangam, three devotional rivers join here; Ganga, Yamuna and Saraswathi. Saraswathi river comes from ground here and this is the holy place in this special moment."

I felt happy and told her, "Great planning for my birthday. Though it is a not full moon, but almost looks like a full moon. Still, few minutes are left for the clock to tick tock to 12:00 am of December 24th."

Only three boatmen and we both were there on the boat. She took the box out from the cover and kept in the middle of the boat, "Three more minutes," said Mythili, "your wish?" "I don't have anything now except you to guide me, I only must believe you," I said. "Cool breeze with moonlight at a devotional place is like an unimagined dream and unexplored fantasy to me." She opened the box and took the cake out. I wasn't able to read what was written on the cake in the moon light. She was trying to light the candle, but due to the breeze in the middle of the river, the candle was not getting lighted. "Few more seconds to twelve," She said and tried to lit the candle. I covered the candle with my hands and sat in the direction of the wind, thus covering the cake. I then asked her, "how will this candle sustain in this wind"?

"This is a sparkling candle, it will stay lit once it is lighted, which would take a few more seconds" She said by checking her mobile. The candle lit and started sparkling. I read what was written on the cake and looked at her with surprise and happiness. "Is this true?" I asked her. She blinked her eyes with a smile, replying, "Yes." "Many Happy Returns to Madan & Mythili." Our date of birth was on the same day and consecutive years. I knew only her birth year, tentatively, but I didn't know about her date of birth. We both looked at each other with those smiling eyes, no, this time we were looking at each other with smiling hearts. My heart was full of happiness, that wintery feel was not making me cold anymore. With that happiness filled in the heart, for the first time, my body was not getting any senses of that happiness inside my heart. Today was the day we both were born and I came to know this feeling that day only, I again asked her, "Is this real? Or you have done this to surprise me? Then she took out her Pan card and passport from her bag and gave it to me. I checked both and 24th December was the date mentioned in both. We cut the cake and celebrated the moment in the best place. That happiness and great feeling continued for almost ten minutes and then I started talking to her and ate the cake. We distributed the cake to those boatmen too, and told them about this surprise also. We spent more than twenty minutes on the boat and returned back. The next morning by 10:00 am, we started towards Varanasi and reached her guest house by 12:30 pm. Back to my guest house, I had lunch, relaxed for a while and joined back in office by 2:00 pm.

Seriously, that day was like an unexplored fantasy from my dreams and an unforgettable memory to us. I was in no mood to work in the office that day, though we were in the office, but my thoughts were still wandering on that boat at Sangam with that cool breeze, celebration, surprise and happy moment of our memory.

One week passed with many happenings and discussions, new year celebrations were done with joy. January 2013 was on the cards now, the focus now shifted to conveying and convincing our parents, as her father was the MD of our company. Mythili needed to deal sensibly without hurting our Egos. Though getting Mythili was important to me, but like everyone, even I couldn't handle my ego when such situations arose with me.

We both went to the temple and took Lord Shiva-Parvathi's blessings in Kashi Vishwanath Mandir and started for Kolkata by flight and she left for her house from the airport whereas I reached Visakhapatnam by train from Kolkata.

After one week:

We met in the Kashi Viswanath temple and she purchased 2

idols of Lord Shiva-Parvathi, and walked inside the temple premises and stood in the queue for darshan. We both didn't reveal to each other about what happened at our home and what could be the conclusion. We both decided last week that whatever would be the decision and conclusion, we would meet at the temple and complete the darshan and after completing darshan, we must first say it to the lord and reveal the conclusion and discussion happened at our home on the temple premises.

We both completed the darshan and came out of the temple but stayed inside the temple premises. Both our eyes were not so much excited, both were clear on conclusion and decision from our respective families, but were not clear about what happened in each other's family. As we came outside the temple and sat in the temple premises, I started looking in her eyes, she was not excited. I asked her, "Why your eyes are not excited and normal, generally your eyes always speak before your heart, I mostly come to know the things from your eyes than your lips,"

She: Excitement, how it can be at this tense moment?

Me: I assumed and understood, that it's a Yes from their side.

She placed one idol of Lord Shiva between us and spelt out with excitement, "It's a Yes, they are convinced on my version and there are no issues and problems in our family," She started explaining what happened in her house and how her father, our MD reacted.

She: (After placing an idol with much excitement) My family accepted this Lord Shiva with his Parvathi.

Me: (I placed a goddess Parvathi idol beside lord Shiva idol) Even my family accepted this goddess Parvathi for this lord Shiva.

Celebrations mode was started, excitement blasted loudly from our hearts to the eyes and we started laughing with excitement. We were looking at our surroundings with happiness, but we couldn't hug inside the temple. Moments of happiness blossom much more in positive places. Though her plan of revealing the conclusion in the temple after darshan made me tensed and worried, but this moment of celebration in such positivity was making us feel blessed. I started looking at her to start this new phase in life in this environment which made us and especially me joyous. Her idea of placing idols and defining our relations as a real blessing was a beautiful moment for both of us. We planned to go for darshan again. After some time, we completed one more darshan and went near the bank of the river. We were just enjoying these moments by visiting all surrounding places to get the maximum positivity in our thoughts.

Happiness was ruling our hearts.

We reached office and joined our work, as work was like something more important that time. After finishing office, we called at our home. Mythili spoke to her father and handed the phone to me.

Uncle: Hi Madan, nice talking to you. Let us meet soon, take care of the things. How are your parents and sister? I hope Mythili conveyed the best news for you guys.

Me: Yes uncle, sorry, yes sir, she told me.

Uncle: Don't worry, you can call me as you like, enjoy. We will meet soon.

Mythili shut the call after some discussion with him. Next, it was my turn. I connected the call to my parents and handed over to Mythili. I didn't know what they were discussing, but I could see the happiness in the eyes of Mythili and got the gist of discussion between them. She continued speaking with my father and sister. I could then sense that happiness from my mother's voice, knowing about her daughter in law and I was very much happy to witness that happiness on a telephone call. Seriously, witnessing the happiness of your mother is the highest from satisfaction in the life of any man.

Blameless Blunder

We continued the celebration of this happiness for the next 5 days. Some staff and colleagues in our office got to know about our relation and acceptance of our proposal by our respective families and thus we were showered with many congratulations and best wishes.

We continued planning the upcoming events and were busy scheduling trips for the next 5 months and other accessories shopping which were required. Finally, we concluded to go back to Kolkata for further shopping and planned a trip to Visakhapatnam to meet our friends, school friends, mutual friends, colleagues and family members. We had to organize many events with these people, we thought to take some good time for marriage and gather all our near ones and in phase by phase, we thought to celebrate this pre-married phase with all good positivity around us with all love. We were thinking much about different ways to explore and enjoy this pre-married phase with pre-wedding photoshoots and evening dates.

We continued our alternate morning visits to the banks of river Ganga and witness the morning sunrise and evening Ganga Arti and Darshan in Kashi Vishwanath mandir daily. We thought to plan one long ride to any other place, as we completed to Allahabad. Now, we were thinking to go to Kolkata by road which was nearly 650 km. However, because as our relation was official, now our parents started to oppose these long rides, since riding a two-wheeler was not an easy task. Therefore, we reached Kolkata by train and met Mythili's parents. Her mother tried to give me good comfort, as that was my first visit to their house. Mythili was their only daughter. After a few minutes, her father joined in our conversation and hugged me with a warm smile in our first meeting. He started narrating his reaction when Mythili told about me and kept the proposal; how he thought about accepting me and what were those best things he heard about me in his enquiry and what he thought before taking this decision to accept it. We continued this discussion for one hour and reached the top floor, went inside the bedroom and then to the balcony.

Our discussion was not on the pace of stopping, we were roaming in the house and continued our discussion. After a while, he opened his almirah and searched for something. In the first place, he didn't get what he was searching for, therefore he searched in other cupboards in his room. There, he got some package with moderate packing, he took it out and removed all the covers in the package, there were a shoe pair inside the package. It was looking like very old, we started looking at that shoe, we both looked at it, but our perceptions were different. I was looking like 'what is this old shoe and why is he taking this and showing me?' Breaking my thoughts, he started a conversation,

He: Madan, what are you thinking about this, can you guess why I took this out?

Me: (Casually, I made a guess) It might be your old shoes or can be your first shoes or some memorable achievement must have been linked to those times when you were using these shoes, thus you kept this here with such care.

He: You are right, Madan, you are almost right, those were the days I started my career and went through many hard phases. I got many achievements later in my career and established an industry, now settled in this empire, but this is the memory and witness of my first steps of starting a career and these are those shoes which walked along with me, crossed many hurdles and witnessed that primary phase success. Do you understand why am I showing this to you, and conveying all this?

Me: Mostly, I can get some similar version from your version as you expect, but I would not take the chance to tell that now. I would love to listen to this from you only.

He: When Mythili told about you, it took 3 hours for us to discuss and to complete her version about you by telling everything. I was in a confused state at that time, but later when I started to enquire and know about you, it took a few minutes to approve you and the content which I heard about you and your thought process and your perception about this life and on our surrounding people made me comfortable and reminded me of my old days. After many years, that was the instance which sent me back to my past and made me feel nostalgic. Then, I felt very happy for accepting you and was proud of Mythili for her selection. I seriously felt you were that person who can walk in my shoes. These are those shoes which witnessed and challenged every situation in my primary phases, I can gift you many great things now, but gifting these shoes is by which I can get the primary satisfaction, this is something where I get emotionally connected.

I was feeling happy, but pressurised at the same time because of such expectations from me. I conveyed the same to him, he just smiled and patted on my shoulders followed by a hug. We went downstairs and saw Mythili and her mother discussing about something. Then, uncle started cracking jokes on them with me and we both were laughing.

Mythili saw us both coming and laughing, she started saying, "I guess that father might have said something about me and my mother; this made you laugh like this, right?"

"Yes," I said.

"I know these instances make my father happy like this, I can sense this by his glowing face, he always takes some time to teasingly comment on my mother. I usually say that an old age teasing case needs to be charged on him," said Mythili and rapid smiles were spread across.

Three days had passed in Kolkata and now I was moving to my hometown Vizag for meeting my parents.

I reached Vizag and started spending time with my family and was involved in many activities like meeting my friends, working from home as and when required, etc. Mythili and I started to fix the dates of our upcoming events of pre-married phase. Back at home, I was also involved with many small works, the days were flying like seconds.

Maybe good times always fly fast or maybe that comfort we take from good times make us feel they fly fast.

A couple of issues got resolved and three days passed. One day, I was in a grocery shop with my sister and she started asking all questions to get that information which she needed about our relation and our mindsets. As she cared for me, she was thinking of all this and we discussed some questions she had. We then continued our shopping to another shopping mall and finished watching a movie followed by shopping of new dresses and accessories and went to the play zone later.

We had some fun time and returned back as it was already 10 pm and shops would have got closed in a few minutes. We reached the parking cellar and I got a call from Mythili telling that she had met with an accident in the morning and she was stable and good now. Listening to this, I went blank and enquired about all the things going on and her wellbeing. I gathered some courage to take this and proceeded on asking her details, I asked her if she was facing any problem while speaking? And told her to not talk more and give the phone to her parents, so that I could discuss about her wellbeing with them.

I was in a hurry of enquiring about every doubt I had about that incident and she explained everything then. She was ok without much injuries, but the impact of the accident seemed high. I was not getting that comfort from her voice perhaps the pain and weakness made her voice much low. I decided to reach Kolkata, the next flight was at 3:30 am. More than 3 hours were left, thus I reached home and packed my bags and started towards the Vizag airport.

I met her father in the hospital and he took me to Mythili. She was sleeping. I saw that big bandage from her stomach to hip, with bloodstains, this made me panic. I felt helpless, and angry, but I was trying to maintain patience, her father noticed my condition and was trying to calm me down by convincing. I didn't have much patience to get convinced without getting to know what actually happened. He said that a broken glass with sharp edge pierced into her stomach and penetrated till her uterus, which resulted in heavy bleeding and there was a huge damage to her uterus with blood loss. This blew my inner soul and I asked him, "how did this happen, how such sharp edge glass piece pierced into her stomach, where did this happen, what she was doing there?

He explained, they (uncle and Mythili) visited their newly constructing house at park street to check the designs. There a worker's son was found playing in sand and concrete used for construction, 20 no. of designer glass pieces which came from Mumbai were unloaded and stacked in a pile kept beside the soil heap in a plan to shift them inside by evening. That kid was playing in soil just beside those glass pieces, the top layer of the pile was a bit inclined downwards and in a condition likely to slip and fall on that kid. Immediately, Mythili ran towards the kid after seeing this and shifted him aside. With the momentum of turning round after shifting that kid, those glass pieces in the top layer of the pile slipped and a sharp-edged piece pierced into Mythili's stomach. We rushed to the hospital immediately carrying Mythili with that penetrated glass piece. Doctors started operating her and removed the glass piece, they noticed heavy bleeding and the uterus had almost damaged. This could result to high chances of not having kids in the future, it's very difficult to bear children for her. They treated her and saved her life after such heavy blood loss, but yesterday night she got a little conscious and she called you and told this.

Me: Does she know about her uterus damage?

He: Yes, she knows that, but her mother doesn't know.

Me: Let's kept this with us only, no one should know this and up to what extent she knows her self-condition?

He: But, Madan.

Me: Nothing more to say uncle, we shall stop this here only. No one apart from us must know this and slowly let's make Mythili also feel she is okay with no problem in her uterus.

He: She knows everything, she boldly took everything yesterday and discussed with the doctor and accepted this hard truth.

Me: Whatever it can and it may be, but let's strictly confine this news amongst us three only. Please don't mind and make sure aunty and my parents also must not know about this. We must stand strong to accept it.

He: Madan, we can tell this to our family members, at least to aunty and your parents. Confining this even before them will not make things right, we are unknowingly cheating ourselves and them. Also, Mythili won't accept this confining before your parents and her mother.

Me: Yes, you are right, I am trying to convince you for not telling this update now. Gradually, we can convey this by seeing the conditions and timing of the upcoming conditions. I feel that an update like this must be shared while considering the conditions, else unknown and invisible disturbances will arise. Also, I know confining this now is not correct, but disturbances which can arise will be comparatively low if we do as I have said.

He: Ok, Madan, I understood, you convinced me, but I don't know how you will convince Mythili.

I gave a smile to him and said, "She is my better half. If one half of me is convinced then the other half will also get convinced. Our connection with souls is in such a way that if we feel it is illogical or incorrect, we won't even think about it, but if we are convinced on any conclusion, we can convince the other half also, uncle," I said this to him and walked away from there to the transparent door of the room where Mythili was taking rest. I was seeing her from outside and thinking of what can be done next, how I must take care of her, how to get rid from such unsafe instincts, how can we create awareness among ourselves and how can we plan the things further.

Imagining her mental strength of taking this, I again get inspired from her as I draw some good inspiration from her every time. Last month, when we planned the long drive trip to Allahabad and she had asked me to come without money and basic necessary things to sustain in this society, that blind belief on her was due to that inspiration and my trust in her. Basically, I don't trust anyone, even if my mind settles with them comfortably, but when Mythili asked me not to carry anything with me, I didn't even hesitate and accepted her proposal to join as she said. That belief in her was now making me recollect my school days of innocent dependence, I started comparing my thought process before and after school days; my state of thought process in college days, issues with bad seeds, leading our rebels, settling issues of those nearby villages to college and then now with this incident.

The doctor came near me to convey that Mythili is conscious now, listening to this word, I rushed to her by maintaining that bold and courageous outer impression. I went inside and sat beside her, held her hands with a smile and by maintaining that patience before her.

She: Sorry Madan, I never thought this would happen. I thought I should rescue that kid and rushed to rescue him.

Me: Don't worry and don't take stress, this type of incident happens at some point or the other. I know, I saw and I thought. Now that's not the issue to discuss, everything is okay and you are out of danger, nothing is of more worth than this to me. Now, you utilize your mind completely to think only of you, don't mis utilize by thinking of the past and future consequences. You are an inspiration to me and let me continue drawing that inspiration from you, you always make me proud with your selfless love.

She: Madan, please don't make me feel uncomfortable; your inspiration is making me uncomfortable; my selfless love is the reason of my condition which can't give you the complete form of our love.

Me: Don't say that, we are just in the initial phases of this incident, many more miracles can come in our way, your positivity will bring all the miracles to us, anything can happen and any improvement can take this to normal. Don't say again about not having the complete form of our love with us, we will definitely have that complete form of our love soon after our marriage, a powerful soul is waiting to join in our lives, we must be steady, healthy and happy now to accept that powerful soul.

She: I Love You, My Madan.

Let's confine this update of your health and uterus between you, me and your father only for now. We can convey this to your mother and my parents gradually by looking at the conditions and their mental state. Let's not make them worried and think much of this. Make yourself ready and healthy. We have so much work to complete before fixing the auspicious time and date of our marriage. Don't think much of the happened past, as I am with you and for you as your better half. There is no meaning in thinking about the past, I believe my other half is strong enough to continue inspiring me.

She started looking at me emotionally after these words and we stopped conversing verbally and started looking at each other silently for a while, these silent conversations between us were very emotional and making our souls feel more comfortable.

(After Three Months)

May 2013

We were engaged on this date in Visakhapatnam. The event was done in the presence of all our near and dear ones, we invited all our school friends and mutual friends, we were showered with many congratulations and best wishes. "You guys are half married now," we turned to our 3'o clock side to see who was that, there was Subbu alias Subbu Lakshmi. We were surprised to see her there, she stated again, "You guys are half married now, congratulations Madan and Mythili. ***Mentally they are completely a married couple and have shared their half with each other"***

"Now, they are marrying for our society," said my father coming behind from Subbu. She greeted my father with a Namaskar, he greeted her and asked us, "Am I correct?"

"Yes, uncle, you are absolutely correct," said Mythili.

Subbu congratulated us, had a photo snap with us and left the stage. After her dispersal, Mythili held and twisted my ears for seeing that glow on my face after seeing Subbu. Subbu was a brahmin girl and one of my childhood crushes along with Mythili and a good mutual friend to both of us. Subbu was the eye witness to that embarrassing situation of my life of misbehaving with Mythili in my childhood at that age of 5 years. I still remember this was that girl who provoked Mythili that I insulted her and made her cry and asked her to shout aloud. She compelled Mythili to complain to my father.

I guess Mythili still remembered all these and twisted my ears after seeing that glow of charm on my face after seeing my old crush. Obviously, that seed of Jealousy was sown in Mythili also, she was nothing less than other women and I conveyed the same to her, she pinched me hard and said, "This is love, not jealousy, you men will never understand this, she continued holding that pinching." "Ok I understood the highest form of love is Jealousy, now stop pinching me," I said.

We completed the event and then involved ourselves in pre-marriage works. We frequently had trips between Kolkata and Vizag. The days were flying with these works; invitations, entertainment, shopping, and we were enjoying this phase. One evening, my father came to me and asked, "Is everything okay?" I said, "Yes." He quietly walked away, I called him back and asked what happened.

He: Mythili told me everything that happened, I am worried about her health and can imagine those situations which you both dealt with and came out of. You both had a very bad time before marriage, you both dealt and came out very nicely with support of each other. This is the real meaning of a relation. Withstanding problems with each other in tough times is a true marriage and you both have reached to that level of understanding before marriage. I feel good and proud of you guys, you guys deserve very best life ahead.

Me: Greatness is all yours, daddy. I grew up witnessing a King like you who treated her Queen with respect and love, what else could be the best lesson for a son on how to treat and understand her lady of life. All the good in my life is only because of you, if there is anything wrong with me in life, then that is completely due to the external world around me and thanks for giving me such a nice foundation in my starting twenty years of life and now I will construct my coming future on that foundation which you have laid in my life, daddy.

Next day, Mythili' s father called daddy and took opinion on different options with marriage dates and finalized our marriage date in *august month, fifteenth date, in nineteenth hour forty-ninth minute* in Visakhapatnam with the venue of the Andhra University Convocation Hall, so our marriage date was August 15th, 2013 at 19:49 hours.

We had a couple of months to complete all our pre-marriage works and invite everyone. We applied for leave in the office and started browsing the internet to get some best designs and check the best works as per our wish to present in the marriage, our special concern was food for all those invites. Seriously, this is a nice phase in everyone's life.

Especially we were enjoying it to the core because we had witnessed and *faced the rough phase of our lives before our marriage. When one half of us got injured, the way another half stood as a support to make the injured half heal, taught us many lessons in understanding and gave freedom to us. Gaining belief from her, I once again thought and realized this basic thing in a relationship between wife and husband;*

Man, always misses that Belief from a woman.

Woman always misses that Freedom from man.

I now got that belief from my other half in our down phase which made me give her the freedom. Mythili had that belief on me due to the way I stood with her in the down phase. The way I thought about her was that she is not the other person in my life, rather she is the other half of me. Treating her as my better half, made her treat me in the same way in her life.

Weds Life

These difficult phases gave us the scope and clarity on providing freedom and having belief on each other. I think if life gives such rough phases before marriage to every couple, then there could not be any high chance of breaking in relations. Non-breaking in relations will lead our social lives and surrounding environment with much positivity which eventually bring a good culture and can stop those marriage fear feelings in youth nowadays. Every rough phase in life will get some good output, but such rough phases to the couples before the marriage will give a good culture in the society and thus, makes a good society, which will be the best change and a good gift to the next generation to continue with.

My father-in-law came to discuss with my father regarding dowry and other gifts to propose before the marriage. My father smiled at him with a respect and said, 3 decades earlier, even my father didn't accept dowry from my mother though my grandfather offered him the dowry. He simply diverted my father-in-law to me by saying, "He is your son-in-law, though we don't have any demands on this, but he may have some demands to fulfil and as a parent we may not know that, so discussion with Madan will give you a better picture on this issue."

My father in-law accepted my father's version in a meaningfully gentle way and came to me, keeping the same proposal of dowry and any other gifts I needed.

Me: Uncle, I believe some sort of mental closeness developed between us during Mythili's accident's phase, with that closeness only I am trying to open up myself on this topic.

He: Sure, Madan, please go ahead.

Me: I respect your views on this topic, but since my childhood, my father always taught me to not accept even his own earned money. I was brought up by him in such a way that I can't even enjoy a plate of biriyani with his money, but I can happily enjoy a glass full of buttermilk with my money. I don't know how far this is correct, but I was brought up in such a way and accepted the life as it came. Even now, I am thankful to my life for giving a genuine girl like Mythili to me as my better half, she is the biggest gift to me from my life. I would request you to spend this dowry amount, which you are thinking to offer to me, to our low salaried family employees in our company instead. I have got Mythili as a beautiful gift in my life, but there may be some other goals of those kids of our low salaried employees, let us gift them their gifts and make their standards of living much better.

He: I am happy and accept your proposal, Madan. I will do the same as you have said, but this is our tradition to offer you this and make your family proud and happy.

Me: My happiness is in the pride of my father and I am sure he will feel proud if we do this. The tradition of this trade can also be done like this, I guess, we may do this trade with the people around us.

He understood and dispersed happily without much conversation.

My sister became a good friend of Mythili, she was a supporting hand in all the pre-marriage activities and I have 3 sister in-laws (cousins of Mythili), who were helping me in deciding all event decorations and event planning work. Though we had many relatives supporting us in this event, but we did not give any major responsibilities to them, as this is our lifetime event, hence we engaged ourselves and decided to take all the load with love and continue the work.

I did all this while continuing with my little office work which I had to complete from time to time.

(August 12th 2013 – 3 days before Marriage)

Things were as per plan till now. Granny of Mythili enters the situation and started disturbing Mythili's mother by creating a big scene in their house by involving Mythili and her parents. Her granny was insisting to stop this marriage event by showing the financial difference as a reason, she started comparing my economic status and predicting Mythili's future in our house after marriage. Though I am economically weaker than her, but it didn't become an issue with anyone till now (till before 3 days of marriage). After hearing this, I felt very happy and excited because we had crossed such phases in our lives and were standing at this moment with much understanding between each other. Now any such silly issues which made Mythili feel bad or guilty would obviously increase her love for me. As expected, uncle started convincing her granny, but she wasn't convinced and he didn't try to spoil her mother's mood. Then Mythili walked towards her politely and started conveying to her about our understanding and the way we took this decision to get married. Also, she conveyed to her that we are that couple who had undergone many tough phases before getting married. She also assured her that how she will manage all the discomforts related to financial issues after marriage and convinced her with her well-mannered confidence, and this issue got resolved without being spread to other family members.

(August 15th 2013 – Auspicious Day)

The auspicious time of the marriage was at 19:49 and as it was in the evening, we had to reach the venue in the morning only for completing other traditional formalities before marriage. We, the groom's side started with a huge *bharaat* to the venue and the bride's side also started with a huge *bharaat* and reached the venue 20 minutes before our bharaat's stipulated time. Almost a thousand people joined in the bharaat and assembled towards the direction of the venue. Many friends, relatives, well-wishers, near and dear ones, colleagues joined the bharaat and enjoyed dancing to the music. It continued for the next 90 minutes and we reached the venue where the bride side came opposite to us and received us with their bharaat. Now the rally became huge and a festive euphoria spread all over at the venue.

In the evening, I got ready for the event and sat on the Kalyan Mandap in the traditional attire, performing puja and greeting all the invitees with a warm smile. The pandit was spelling out shlokas and mantras and making me perform some puja. The photographers were covering the event with utmost dedication. Then, there came the bride in a decent traditional costume and simple ornaments. The other ladies surrounding her for bringing her till Kalyan Mandap were heavily decorated with heavy designer wears and heavy gold ornaments. Mythili, in the middle was looking very simple, beautiful, and realistic amongst all those ladies. Though she didn't prefer heavy dressing and ornaments, but her charm and royal made her so special in the event.

Till now, I had witnessed and heard of many marriages in life where the bride dominates everyone with all designer wears and heavy ornaments, but for the first time, that too in my wedding, I was looking at my better half, dressed simply, which drew my heart once again to get inspired from her. She came on the Kalyan Mandap and after a few minutes the pandit made her sit beside me. The first few words I have spoken to her on this day were, "Why is this so simple without any showcase of ornaments and makeup on this special day of ours. Though, I love this, but I didn't understand what made you change, that too after our many planning."

"I can easily make myself ready with heavy ornaments and a good designer dress, but I didn't find the truth in those.

This is such a special moment of my life which will make me start a new life with the real you, My life, My Moments will turn into Our life and Our moments. Such is the reality I realized in this event, sharing a life by becoming a better half of a real honest person like you is true dress on me and filling my heart with your love is the true ornament I would ever wear," She said.

This blew me again. With much emotion and love for her, I proudly and happily took a deep breath and continued enjoying that pride with her and waited for that auspicious minute which would make her my better half.

Bringing me out from this moment, my father-in-law sat before me with a plate and water in a silver bucket. The pandit asked me to keep my legs in that plate as my father in law will wash my legs which is a ritual of marriage. He, along with my mother-in-law started washing my feet and started saying his feelings from his heart to both of us,

"You both are such a good pair who can even inspire yesterday's generation with your maturity & support for each other

You both are desire and manifestation of Love. Everything in your relationship is your understanding and hard work

Your past is the language of love and You must be the way of Love."

He completed this ritual with these heavy and lovely words which made us emotional. Continuing these emotions, the pandit rearranged our seating just opposite to each other, as there were only a few minutes more to that auspicious time of *Muhurath*. I called my mother and sister near me and told them, "I Love You" with a kiss. All our near and dear ones surrounded us with those rice grains mixed with turmeric and ghee. A lifetime moment was just seconds away. The pandit handed that Jaggery and Jeera mixed paste in a betel leaf which I kept on Mythili's head and Mythili kept in my head at that minute.

After that, the Pandit asked to do the ritual and the music band played a marriage tune. We both were officially one, our halves exchanged with much love. I tied those three knots to her, "Welcome to my Life, Mythili, now you are Mythili Madan," I said to her. She smiled and replied with a kiss on my forehead, saying, "I LOVE YOU." We both were feeling and enjoying this moment of our lives.

We settled side by side and people were standing in a line to bless us. I saw a couple standing in the line. I had seen them somewhere else before, but was unable to recollect them clearly and asked the same to Mythili. She called them and introduced them to me by saying, "He is Mr. Krishna, our distributor from Vizag sales office, he recently joined our team and now he is here to bless us." I was trying to recollect him.

Meanwhile, Mr. Krishna started saying, "I didn't have much scope in marketing, but Mythili was like my daughter who came to me and explained everything and by changing some regulations feasible to me, she allowed to associate with this company by doing business with good profit. I came with my family here to bless this good-hearted God gifted daughter," I was trying to recollect this familiar face from my past. One more girl came and stood beside him, she was Jhansi (sister of Mrudhula). She came to us with a warm smile and congratulated us. This blew my mind and made my heart heavy and emotional. I was trying to smile and come out of this situation. Mythili placed her hand on my shoulders and explained everything; after our marriage was fixed, she went searching for Mrudhula's family and found they were facing financial troubles, so she gave Mr. Krishna an opportunity to do business with our company. No one knew about this happening; this was the first blow out she gave me after marriage.

Me: I don't know how to react and I am speechless, thanks for this Mythili, I didn't even imagine this, you not only performed my dharma as yours, you also balanced my Karma by supporting them.

She: I am your half, I accepted you doesn't mean I accept your present and future, I also accepted your past and did this as our responsibility.

It took almost three hours to complete the line of blessings and two more hours to complete all other puja rituals in the event. After 6 hours, it was time to take Mythili with us and we would be taking her to our home. This is the most emotional time in every girl's life, here emotions dance without any music, here emotions swim in the tears, here emotions drench the heart. Mythili's parents (my in-laws) along with me started walking to my parents in the event hall, then the emotion riddles started in my mother's eyes with happiness of accepting Mythili and taking her into our family, my sister started a row of tears and made emotions swim.

My father stepped ahead with confidence of handling the situation and started conveying to my in-laws the best assurance of happiness and taking great care of Mythili. Mythili's parents were just listening to my father's words and felt that warm support in this emotional ride. My mother-in-law burst out her emotions and opened that tap of tears by holding Mythili and keeping her hand in my hand with an unspoken message of 'take care.' My father along with my mother came forward and held our hands (Mythili's hand in my hand) and started convincing them (my in-laws) gently.

"Pride of any father of a daughter always lies in his daughter only. Mythili is such a daughter and aspiring woman who makes you proud always, we are happy to join her in our family and will take care of her well-being along with us," said my father to my father-in-law and assured by filling confidence in them.

After 20 minutes, we completed all the rituals and started from the location, and reached our house in a few more minutes.

Belief & Freedom

It took one week to complete the remaining rituals after marriage in my house. Living a life with my lady, my wife, my love so closely 24 hours was a great feeling. This was the new phase of life we both were experiencing. As she was the girl who came from one house to another house, she had many emotions, sentiments, differences in daily lifestyle comparatively. She experienced many differences as things were different in both the houses and lifestyles. And of course, every woman must have experienced this, but I was concerned about my woman. I along with my family will take much care of her wellbeing. I personally have a thought to give much freedom to her because

I believe women with wings fly higher than rockets with their dreams and aspirations.

Mythili was one of such rare kind of woman I ever witnessed, she is capable enough of handling any situations and balancing the relations with good emotions and belief.

Every woman has some or the other kind of resistance with the in-laws; mother-in-law and sister-in-law at in-laws' home after marriage. I witnessed these kinds of differences in many families, where the newly married woman is not able to balance. I was just thinking and waiting to witness how Mythili will overcome this challenge, though I had a belief on Mythili and she had enough freedom to manage the relations. Still, the course of action to witness was awaited. The days were flying to weeks, weeks flying to months, a couple of months passed, Mythili got good acceptance in our house. I was trying to search those loopholes in relations of Mythili with my family and relatives. Though she can handle good business relations and has good IQ, can manage situations better in her favour, her way of receiving love from our family members made me get inspired once again from Mythili. As I said I was waiting to witness, the course of action on how she would excel in this phase where most successful women also fall into the trap of issues, but the way Mythili got a good acceptance was just amazing and wonderful. Though she was the girl from a good and better-lived family than ours, though they were economically stronger than us, the way Mythili moulded herself in our family made me realize the way she was brought up in her family. Her behaviour defined her family status in tradition; very well behaved and well-mannered. They brought up their child in such a way that she was able to mould her lifestyle conveniently with much ease.

Her adjusting from that villa to our double bedroom house.
Her relations from the owner of company to a member of the family.

Her planning from those billions to our lakhs of budget.

Her complaint-less behaviour from leading to dealing.

Her handling of thousand stockholders to a few family members.

Her welcoming attitude to mingle and going ways.

Her greatness to our simplicity.

She never expected the things, rather she planned the ways of achieving the things. She was loved by all, she maintained good relations and honest talks with every member of the family, she thought and planned about every member of the family, she guided and suggested changes in lifestyles of our family members. Keeping that result apart, her involvement in guiding and suggesting changes impressed everyone. She never had a complaint about anyone, even in her eyes, on dealing and working on household activities, she was completely involved in her way of mingling with our family and was trying to create a better, progressive environment in our family. She, of course, brought that realization of our mistakes in our lifestyles where we were facing issues with and the way she sensibly dealt with the stubborn mindset persons like our grandpa and granny was completely outstanding, she changed their perception on life and family relations without touching their ego and respect. Mythili touched their hearts. From her experiences in life, she was able to bring change in our lifestyles and our family members started believing her approach and gained belief on her actions and intentions which resulted in a good acceptance in family and society.

There were some situations where she used to get stuck between the ego of different mindset people in the family and became the middle line between both mindsets and tried to solve the situations sensibly. Keeping apart the solution of those issues between multiple mindsets, her trying and concern on reducing such aroused differences made everyone feel good which resulted in improving her acceptance and weightage of her words.

Many examples can define her maturity and moulding herself into our family by changing the mindsets of our elders; grandpa and granny.

Our family was looking for a well settled match in our community for my sister, whereas my sister was having another guy in her heart who was from other community. This was the cold burning topic in our family for last three years, but the way Mythili convinced everyone in our family by her logics of tomorrow's generation, parallelly giving importance to yesterday generation, was commendable.

Except my grandfather, everyone in the house was convinced by her logic and thought process of accepting my sister's proposal. Generally, brothers in every house get married after the younger sister's marriage, but due to this issue, I got married before my sister, she convinced both of us to get married before her marriage. Mythili took this as her concern and tried her best to sort out the issue in favour of my sister. Mythili judged both versions in my family and decided to support my sister where she was alone without much support from the family. Mythili convinced everyone in a couple of months for marriage, but only my grandfather was rigid on this and asked Mythili to stay away from the matter. This rude statement became an issue with everyone in the family because everyone was concerned towards Mythili. This continued for a couple of weeks in the family, where all our family members gradually started supporting Mythili. It hurt the ego of my grandfather as he was the one who controlled our family since starting and till then no one opposed his words, but now for the sake of Mythili and her genuineness, every other person in the family started opposing my grandpa in his back end.

Mythili understood this inclination of emotions in our family and tried to balanced emotions of my grandpa very tactfully by giving him utmost importance for his every decision and keeping his version as prime in every conclusion. This went for a couple of months. Finally, after six months of our marriage, Mythili succeeded in getting acceptance for my sister's marriage as per my sister's wish. The three years cold war on this issue concluded after getting acceptance from my grandfather. Now, all our family members were in one version of my sister's marriage.

Her thinking on financial planning of our family was one more example of keeping our family in a better position and by gaining the acceptance of her words, she changed her lifestyle in such a way that spending lakhs of rupees for managing was brought down to thousands of rupees perfectly. If she wanted, she could have brought those lakhs and would have spent as she liked, but she planned everything in such a way that her lakhs were reduced to a few thousands and our budget got a proper planning and spending. This cautionary and vigilant nature on spending money impressed everyone.

I never thought our family could have many such good changes which actually improved our lifestyle.

I only married a girl and gave her freedom to explore things; freedom without any restrictions and relation without any hidings can make our married life beautiful, this is what I realized. I continued to witness the lifestyles in my surrounding globe where people were celebrating their relations with luxury, fake visions, fake credits, celebration modes, unpractical praising and giving fake credits. Anyway, all these were not at all constructive in any of their lifestyles.

The most common difference I witnessed in other relations and my relation was Belief and Freedom, nothing to fake, sharing everything with her without any hidings and subsequently receiving the same genuine behaviour from her end.

I realized that the meaning of accepting her as my better half is not only in my thoughts, but also in our life styles. After witnessing her good acceptance and changes in the thought process of my family, I believe that this could be the best result we could have from our life partner.

There are many such examples of changes that happened after our marriage. Living with her so closely brought the realization in my IN ME about the basic mistake others were making. Also, our experience of facing tough times before our marriage corrected us.

Belief on Man of a Woman, Belief on Husband of a Wife

(if this is established by sharing their souls with each other)

and

Freedom to Women from man, Freedom to Wife from Husband

(If this is established as a belief between two souls),

then one can have a better family without many disturbances. Of course, the bond of Wife & Husband gets stronger with quarrels and fights only, but the quality and intent of the quarrels and fights makes the difference. If we have this Belief & Freedom on each other, then we can lead a quality, peaceful and progressive life.

Sharing the souls is not like sharing ourselves nakedly with each other physically, but sharing everything in us without a piece of secret. This sharing of souls is the other form of being the best halves to each other.

Best halves will never have silly quarrels which are unhealthy in their relation and quite commonly noticeable in most of the relations these days.

(February 1st 2016, clock tick-tocks to 05:30 pm in Visakhapatnam)

It was almost 2 and half years after our marriage, our travelling in life till then was like sailing in a ship on sea with pleasant ups and drastic downs. Yes, we faced severe health issues where the problem cornered Mythili few times in pregnancy and challenged her mental strength. Still, we overcame it by standing with each other and working and travelling to our other branches in India and then settling ourselves in Visakhapatnam.

We were in our house with snacks bucket in our hand, my father was giving me a bowl of popcorn to have, we were watching television and other music and news channels randomly and spending the evening, even my in-laws were in our house, they came to Visakhapatnam on a business conference and came to our house as Mythili was a 9th-month pregnant lady then. Yes, Mythili was 9 months pregnant and expected to conceive next month.

From last 2 and half years after our marriage, she conceived twice and aborted once because of some problem in her uterus. This time with necessary tests and analysis of her uterus condition during the first aborted phase, we followed the doctor's instructions very well to avoid further level of consequences. We planned after necessary medication, but still, risk was present even in the 9th month also. Very carefully, we maintained our living standards to have a delivery in next 25 days.

This was a very crucial time for both of us and for the baby in her womb. In this condition, we were well prepared and prayed for the days to pass normally by taking all those precautions.

The clock tick tocks to 09:00 pm, as usually we were watching news bulletin at 9 pm and preparing to settle in the dining table for dinner. There was a news about some riots which happened due to some communal clashes. Some of father's friends were in the house and my in-laws were also watching this news, they were involved in discussing this news in our hall. I was having my dinner in our dining room and listening to all those discussions to know the gist and the different versions on such clashes in our surrounding world. This discussion went on till 10:00 pm. Meanwhile, I finished my dinner and sat with them to continue listening to what happened. Mythili had also finished her dinner and went to sleep in our room, as everyone knew how a pregnant lady in her 9th month sleeps. She was not comfortable and free to have a good position on the bed as those tiny baby kicks from inside her womb caused trouble. As I was involved in listening and discussing about those riots, she slept without disturbing me from that conversation taking place in our hall with my father, his friends and in-laws. I went to check what she was doing. It was 11:30 pm, she was in deep sleep and I didn't turn on the light in our room and slept beside her.

I was in deep sleep and sensed some scratching on my hand while sleeping, but unable to come out of my sleep, I didn't notice. After a while, I heard some sounds beside me. Gradually, I came into this world from my sleep. Suddenly, lights were turned on in our room which disturbed my sleep and brought me into this world. My mother stood before our bed and I asked her what happened. Parallelly, I looked by my side, Mythili was slowly shouting in pain and closed her eyes and held the bedsheet tightly with her hands. My mother understood the seriousness and started supporting and massaging her. I quickly ran to my father and in-laws sleeping in other rooms of our house and told them the situation. I asked them to run fast into our room, I called the ambulance and consulted our family doctor and explained the condition in a hurried tone. I then felt a little comfortable as everyone in my house were around her and trying their best to support her.

My father came to me and said, "at this time you must stay beside her, I will take care of all this and coordinate with the hospital and other support services we require." "You go and stay with Mythili," he said.

I ran to our bedroom and sat beside her and began consoling her with moral boost up. My father took our car out from the garage and asked me and my father in-law to shift Mythili carefully by holding the bedsheet and pillow into the car to take her to the hospital.

Present Day

(Around 05:00 am on 02.02.2016)
this is where the story started

Doctor completes her preliminary check-up and conveys about the condition being critical, either mother or baby can be saved, or in other case we may lose both. This makes me to fall on my knees, I cannot take this, I am shocked to listen to this. Many supporting hands come on my shoulders as a support, trying to console me by saying that nothing wrong will happen, stay strong. People are trying to boost my morale, but everything that happened in life starts running in my mind, starting from Mrudhula's episode to now Mythili.

I am not ready to take this anymore in life.

I couldn't take this and I will not take this in my life. Maybe I will be at a stage to take and manage this in life, but definitely, I will not take this condition now. It took me few years to come out from the tragedy happened with Mrudhula and now Mythili, if any bad happens to Mythili, then I will not at all take this. These thoughts are burning, running and kicking hard in my IN ME.

A lot of mesh is created around me and the information about Mythili has spread to all our relatives. They are reaching the hospital to console me. My father is the only person with me and giving enough moral by reminding me the strength of Mythili and what she achieved. In this situation, I am not even able to recollect all those positives or strengths of my wife.

The doctor comes to me and asks to sign on that declaration form before starting the operation. "As this is 9th month of her pregnancy", the doctor says, "we will try to save both baby and mother, but in worse, whom should we give the preference to save first?" Tears roll down my eyes before doctor Ayesha, I am not able to control myself and then hold the hands of Doctor Ayesha and I say, "*My Mythili is my Life, she is my everything, I am no more without her, I don't want anything in this world without Mythili. Please make her normal send her back in normal condition to me, I say this with tears in my eyes.*

She understands and walks away to the operation theatre. I never prayed to God in my life till now or thought of asking for some support from God till now, in my tough phases also I tried to stand hard and take the kick from life and took support from the people behind me, but now in this situation, I kneel before God and start praying and asking to give back my Mythili in normal condition without any risk to her life ever.

My father and mother both come to me and hug me tightly and start consoling me, trying to build my moral by saying,

"Hey, idiot, you are a stubborn guy, who crossed infinite hurdles in life and stood successfully & married your lovely lady,

Yes, she is your wife, she loves you & you love her.

You know how strong she is,

Did she ever quit any war?

Whoever be the opponent, Is she an easy lady for the opponent to win?

You have the world's strongest wife with you,

The more you get tense, the more you are degrading your wife, You are the power of the world, but she is the power in you.

These words hit my heart and give some confidence to me to breathe and give some time to the life with hope and I start walking alone to the other corner of this hospital and sit on this chair which made me to think all that happened in my life and how I crossed these ups and downs.

How I took inspiration from my wife, How we both started our relation,

How we stood together for each other,

How she stood in my tough times,

How I stood in her tough times,

How she became my half,

How we tried to understand this life,

How we looked at the things out of the box,

How she changed my perception about everything to positive,

How she made me feel humiliated with her love

(Thirty Minutes later)

Doctor Ayesha is walking towards me by removing her hand gloves. I guess the operation is completed, but I am unable to sense clearly on what happened. All my guess powers are getting failed seeing her walk from the operation theatre towards me and tension starts inside me with what version she is coming to me and what could she say. She comes to me and says, **"Both are Safe."**

I am continuing in that trance now and ask her, "What?"

"Yes, Mr. Madan, don't worry, **you and Mythili are blessed with a baby girl, both mother and baby are safe now**, no risk or life threatening to both, we tried our best to save both mother and baby and we have succeeded in that."

I fall on my knees and start showing my gratitude by thanking her.

After six hours of observation, both baby and mother are shifted to a room from observation point. I walk inside with shivering hands and sweat on my body. Those tiny legs are visible in a cradle beside Mythili's bed. I am walking inside, though there is my better half, Mythili, looking towards me with a smile, I unknowingly ignore her without any reason and walk towards my daughter. I took her carefully in my hands and start blushing by seeing her and feeling her in my hands. Still, time is not permitting me to look at Mythili. My IN ME splits now and I start speaking. My heart is comfortable in continuing to look at my daughter whereas my mind is insisting to look and talk to Mythili, but I continue looking at my daughter only. After such a tough phase, the relaxation which my heart is feeling right now is priceless and for the first time in my life, my IN ME is separated and continuing inside me with two different versions. My mind is on Mythili and Heart is on my daughter and my eyes following my heart.

Few minutes later, I keep my daughter back in the cradle and look into the eyes of Mythili. We are just silent and smiling at each other, we don't have anything to converse among us, this continues for a minute between us.

I am rechecking my version of ignoring the only important relation in my life (my half). Now, I start looking at my daughter. I don't know why this is happening, but this is good and we both are comfortably accepting this change without any conversation among us. This is an example for me on manifesting the level of understanding we have. After a while, Mythili asks me,

She: Are you afraid?

Me: Yes.

She: Why, do you love me that much? Doctor Ayesha told me that you gave the preference to save me, but now have started loving our daughter more than me?

Me: (smiling on her question coming from jealousy) I don't know.

She: What do you know then?

Me: I look at my past in your thoughts, I witness our future in your smile and I feel that devotion in your eyes.

I witnessed those 9 basic emotions of life in your eyes:

I witnessed ***Love*** in your eyes now when I ignored you & went towards our daughter.

I witnessed ***Heroism*** in your eyes when you stepped ahead to save that boy in your apartment from that glass, without any second thought.

I witnessed ***Terror*** in your eyes when we both sat at Kashi Vishwanath temple to reveal the decisions of our families about our marriage with 2 idols of lord Shiva & Parvathi.

I witnessed ***Anger*** in your eyes for Subbu when she came to our engagement and started showering some love on me.

I witnessed ***Joy*** in your eyes when I teased you indirectly at a restaurant in Varanasi.

I witnessed ***Sadness*** in your eyes when doctors said we may not have kids in future due to that accident and cut on your uterus.

I witnessed ***Wonder*** in your eyes when you started explaining how you explored me from that art exhibition (when you saw me again).

I witnessed ***Disgust*** in your eyes when you were recollecting those childhood incidents where I misbehaved with you.

I witnessed ***Peace*** in your eyes always because you are always at peace. Without peace, you could not make this possible.

I am conveying these priceless feelings to Mythili and am enjoying by looking at that magic of love in her eyes. Unknowingly, my eyesight shifts to my daughter sleeping in the cradle beside Mythili. She is just looking at me with her little opened eyes and chubby pink cheeks. I become voiceless after getting those love arrows from her eyes and this is something only a man who got dominated by his daughter's love more than his wife's love, can relate to and understand.